ABDUCTED

ALEXIS ABBOTT

PATHFORGERS PUBLISHING

Want to keep up to date with all my new releases, sales, and giveaways? What about getting a **Free** bad boy romance novel? Subscribe to my VIP Reader List:

http://alexisabbott.com/newsletter

*H*e's getting closer.

At first I think it's all in my head, that I'm just imagining the footsteps behind me picking up speed to match my pace as I walk to the bus stop. But my heart is pounding, because I'm all alone, and there's a man behind me. Following me.

I just finished my Saturday night shift at the sports bar where I work weekends. It's a few minutes before midnight and the sky is dark, nearly pitch-black, punctuated only occasionally by the greenish glow of a streetlamp overhead. But this is the seedy side of town, and most of the streetlights are burned out. When things go wrong, big or small, on this side of the railroad tracks, the city doesn't care to fix it.

Those of us who live over here are so far down the list of priorities, we might as well not exist.

So I've gotten used to it. The rushed half-jog to the bus stop after work in the eerie darkness. Sometimes, when I'm lucky, I can convince one of my male coworkers to walk me there as protection. Most of the guys at the sports bar are tall, broad-shouldered. Former high school athletes and bouncers.

Those types.

But tonight, my usual escort was busy flirting with some girl at the bar. Whatever. That was his prerogative. I'm sure they got tired of walking me to the bus stop and never getting more than a hug and a smile of gratitude in return. And that's how it is in this world: you get what you give. So tonight I thought it would be okay, just this once, for me to make the long walk myself.

Except I was wrong.

This is not okay.

Someone is behind me, following me, and has been for at least five or six minutes. And now that he's keeping up with me, his footsteps matching mine as I break into a jog, I know it's serious. It is no coincidence that we happen to both be on the same route in the middle of the night. He's trailing me and I have nowhere to go.

Terror grips my heart as I try to pick up the pace, my feet aching with every quickened step.

For my job at the sports bar, I'm required to wear high heels that "make my ass and calves look good," according to my sleazy boss, Howie. And that's all well and good when I'm in the bar. I can walk in heels, no problem. But this is Rochester, New York. It's the ninth of December, and it's snowing like crazy. Usually I bring a pair of snow-friendly boots to change into, but tonight I was almost late for work and had to rush. So now I was dashing through the snow in four-inch heels, my feet freezing and my heart pounding, because holy hell, there is someone chasing me!

I glance back over my shoulder and see a tall, thin figure following after me. He's jogging with a slight stoop, like his back isn't quite straight. Maybe an older guy? But what kind of old man chases young women down the street at midnight?

I trip over a chunk of ice on the sidewalk and go flying, landing on my knees, skidding across the snow and ice with a little shriek of terror. It hurts like hell, my work pants soiled and tearing at the knees. "Shit," I cry out as I push my hands into the freezing cement, hurrying to get back on my feet.

My follower is running now, trying to take advantage of my fall.

Adrenaline pumps through my veins, pushing me on. I jump up and kick off my heels, then break into a flat-out run down the street. I'm only wearing tights under my pants and a pair of thin socks, so my feet are aching with the cold underneath.

My lungs burn with every breath of chilly air, my

knee throbbing, my head pounding with fear. What does he want from me? Is he trying to mug me? Or... worse?

I am not about to find out. It's only another block now to the bus stop. I can make it.

My feet are starting to go numb and I'm losing my traction, sliding on the squeaky snow and icy pavement in my sock feet, but I keep on running. No matter how much it hurts, no matter how many pebbles and stones and ice shards stab my bare feet, I'm not going to be captured by the terrifying man!

But my heart nearly stops as I see the bus up-ahead, pulling away from my stop. It's come early. Just by a few minutes, but early enough that I'm going to miss it. Not only is that my ride home, it's my only chance of escape from the man chasing me. The other people that would be waiting there my only hope of help.

"No, no, no!" I cry out, tears blurring my vision I leap over a big shoveled-up pile of snow and go sliding again.

"Please! Wait! Come back!" I scream out, my voice sounding ragged as I struggle to keep my breathing even. The bus is picking up speed, oblivious to my desperate plight, while the man behind me gains momentum.

I look back again and shout, "Leave me alone, you creep! I have mace!" I lie, trying to fumble with my purse, like I really might put out his eyes with pepper spray.

He doesn't answer. He's dressed in all black, the hood of his puffy jacket pulled over his forehead far enough to cast his entire face in shadow. I can tell from his slightly hobbling gait that he is, in fact, an older guy. But that's about all I can figure out. And for an old man, he sure seems to be in pretty damn good shape, keeping pace with me.

No. More than that. He's gaining on me.

I look around frantically, wondering where I can go to hide. Even though I live and work on this side of town, I don't have a lot of friends nearby. Well, actually, I have almost no friends. I keep to myself. And with how many hours I work between my two jobs and overnight nursing classes, I don't have time to build relationships. Which means I don't know anyone in these apartment buildings.

The police station is blocks and blocks away. There are no retail businesses in the neighborhood. I have nowhere to go. I turn and see a long, dark alleyway to my left. Before I can second-guess the decision I bolt in that direction. I don't know what my plan is. I don't know what I'm going to do. The only thing in my head is this voice clanging over and over again: RUN. RUN. RUN. DO NOT STOP FOR ANYTHING.

As soon as I run into the shadows of the alleyway, I cry out in pain as something sharp pierces through my sock and through the numb sole of my right foot. Tripping, instinctively babying my right foot, I fall to one side and slam into a brick wall, then crumple down to the freezing cold ground. In the faint light, I can make out hundreds of glittering glass shards from a shattered bottle of malt liquor. I wiggle back against the wall next to a stinking dumpster, cradling my right foot, which is bloody and searing with pain and cold. I try to blend into the darkness, hoping my assailant won't find me, by some miracle.

He comes bolting into the alley and looks around, breathing heavily. My heart is pounding so loud I fear it might give me away. It's like an overwhelming rushing sound in my ears. Surely he can hear it. Surely he can smell me. Smell my fear.

He walks slowly along, looking from side to side. As he approaches, he kicks the glass shards with his heavy boot, and some of the glass comes flying my way, clattering against the dumpster.

His breathing gets closer, deep and steady, as if he didn't just chase me at full speed for two blocks. He's calm, toying with me.

He kicks more glass, closer to the dumpster, and with two more steps, he's going to see me.

Crunch goes the glass under his heavy boots, his pace slow as I shiver in the snow, trying to hold my breath, trying not to give myself away. A light buzzes to my left, as if struggling to emit light, keeping us both in the dark until a small flash of dim, overhead light gives me the sight of him.

He's huge, his body imposing and terrifying, and I catch just a hint of his malicious grin which turns my heart cold.

He's spotted me.

He reaches for me and I fumble around for a weapon of some kind. I desperately grab a larger chunk of sharp glass and begin flailing at him with it, shrieking as he wrestles to get to me. I kick at him with both feet, screaming.

"Help! Help me, please! Somebody!" I wail, tears burning on my cold cheeks.

I get a few good swipes in with the chunk of glass, but my attacker is wearing too many layers. I can't even actually cut him. It's so dark and I'm so exhausted, my whole body freezing cold. My feet ache. One of them is bleeding. The man grabs me by the shoulders and slams me back against the brick wall, my head bursting with pain and dizziness.

"Don't," I sob weakly. "Please." My mind racing with a million thoughts of what happens to young women in dark alleyways when at the mercy of cruel men.

Somewhere it occurs to me that something smells like the hospital. Like the ward where I once shadowed an instructor for nursing school. What is it? What is the smell? It's slightly sweet and cloying.

It makes my nose wrinkle even as the world falls dark around me.

Tapioca. It's tapioca.

And then something else is pressed against my face, my nose and my mouth. I try to suck in a deep breath, but when I do, the alley falls away and everything goes black.

Mercy is not an emotion I feel.

I stalk through the smoky living room of the penthouse apartment, listening to the sound of the rain pattering against the windows over the low, pained groaning on the ground.

There's a gun in my hand, one bullet left, and the blood spilled from the other five is on my hands, literally. It's also staining my black clothes and running in thin streams on the tile floors. I loom over the carnage in the room like the Grim Reaper himself, my dark eyes scanning the bodies on the ground for signs of life.

Two of the men never made it out of their seats and lie slumped on the table. One got up to run, and his brains are splattered on the wall-length windows. The man who was coming out of the bathroom has his throat slashed open, slumped over the corpse of the one man who had been fast enough to draw his gun and try to shoot at me before I blasted his hand off and put a second bullet in his heart.

The doorman lies behind me, his one eye open and staring as blood runs out the knife-hole I put in the other eye.

A minute ago, the apartment had been full of some of the most powerful men in my corner of New York City, enjoying a pleasant evening with drinks and probably a little chatting about work. They were men who trusted me. Men who paid me. Men who relied on me.

And I just slaughtered them like the pigs they are.

Even as I approach the one survivor who is slumped against the wall, blood running from the shot in his gut, agony on his face, I feel no remorse. No regret.

The glassy look in his eyes tells me that his vision is getting blurry. Fear comes over his face as he realizes I'm approaching him, and I can see him fighting to stay awake.

"Y... you," he struggles to say, disbelief in his voice. *"Angel of Death."*

My title.

My six and a half feet of height looms over his form, clad in a matching black turtleneck, leather jacket, leather gloves, jeans, and shoes. My eyes that these very men have called *blacker than a moonless night* glare down at him.

"I... please," he croaks, trying and failing to raise a hand to me.

I look at his meaty hand covering the hole in his stomach, hearing the disgusting squelch of blood as his hand twitches and he winces. He'll bleed out in a matter of minutes without medical attention.

"Anything," he says in a hoarse whisper. "Money... women... power?"

I simply move my head side to side, my face still as a statue.

They should know better than to bargain with me, after everything they've had me do, after knowing about every soul who has begged me for mercy in the past.

And they all begged for their lives more convincingly than these people.

The only question on my mind is whether to put him down now, or let him suffer.

At my silence, his lip quivers, and he gives his head a feeble shake before managing a final sentence.

"At least... tell me why."

I raise my pistol, aiming it at his paunchy face, right between the dull, piggish eyes. My mind is made up. Not even the satisfaction of letting these pigs feel pain is worth leaving loose ends. My reputation is well-earned.

"No," is the only word I give him before I pull the trigger, and a final silenced shot fires. I watch his body twitch for a second when the fresh hole appears in his head, and then, all is still.

As silently as I came in, the Angel of Death sweeps out of the building, not a soul spotting me in or out.

My sleek, black car tears down the highway like a shadow over the next four hours. Soon, the great glowing lights of New York City are shrinking behind me as I head northwest, upstate.

Streetlights flash by me overhead through the windshield. I catch a glimpse of the shining blood still on my leather gloves. At a gas station halfway through my journey, I take them off along with my jacket and seal them in a bag in the back of the car. I'll dispose of them later, with the rest of these clothes. I have several outfits identical to it in a small suitcase in the trunk. I slip on a less intimidating red hat and big fishing glasses, and I go inside to buy a coffee and a little food with cash. I don't want to be obvious to the cameras.

I wonder how long it will be before they come looking for me—either the police or the mafia.

I won't be going back to New York City anytime soon. Maybe not ever.

Finally, hours after midnight, I get off the highway and am soon driving through the woods and poorly lit roads.

I pass a sign for Seneca Falls, a deer with one antler standing frozen beside it as my car blazes by.

It's a small, sleepy town south of Rochester, not the kind of place people bother to stop very often.

And it's going to be my home for a while.

After a short time, I turn off onto a dirt road, and halfway to my destination, I pull the car to the side of the road and turn it off.

This will be the only night I can't bring the car all the way down the road.

I will need to be stealthy just one more time tonight.

Even though I'm used to smooth streets, my footsteps are silent as I stalk down the gravel road for half a mile. There's the faintest bit of moonlight to guide my way. I move through the woodland road like I was born on it.

Sometimes, I wonder if my nickname isn't a coincidence. Maybe I am god's own Angel of Death, visiting this world to bring the end to people whose time has come.

I've done my job efficiently all these years. So efficiently that even if I were an angel, I doubt that my massacre tonight could wash away my sins.

A crack of a smile comes across my dark face. Maybe this world is my hell.

Finally, I come to my goal at the end of the winding road.

It's a big white farmhouse that looks like it might be abandoned. It's old, but that just proves how sturdy it is. There's a barn in the backyard that's even more run-down than the house, and I can only guess it was turned into a shed years ago and forgotten.

I crouch down and move up to the house, low to the ground. There's a light on in the kitchen, but that doesn't tell me anything: it could mean the owner is awake, or it could mean he just left the lights on.

I slip up to what I imagine is the bedroom window, and I peer inside. There's enough light coming from the hallway to show me the bed is empty. Carefully, I put my hands on the window and push up slowly.

It slides up.

Over the years, I've found "house call" jobs relatively easy. I'm amazed by how often people leave windows unlocked, forget to set alarms, or even forget to lock the front door at night. I'm surprised that this particular man has slipped up like that, but out here in the middle of nowhere, I can see how it's easy to let your guard down.

My toned arms push me up through the window with ease, and I enter the room without a sound.

I look around and see a simple room with little decor. There is trash on the dresser, and I frown in disgust at the wads of tissue littering the floor. Apparently, this man has been living alone so long he doesn't care to even clean up after jerking off. My brow knits in anger as I see pictures on the bed of girls far too young.

The sound of bubbling water down the hall gets my attention, and I hear the sound of someone moving in the kitchen.

I take out my gun.

Every step I take down the hall is silent, despite the old wooden floors. I stick close to the wall, where I'm less likely to make noise, and I know how to watch floorboards for signs that they might creak. Every step is measured, every move of my muscles is perfectly honed from years of experience.

I am a contract killer, a hunter of men, and I'm damn good at my job.

I take out a mirror from my pocket and use it to look around the corner into the kitchen. I see an old man with shoulder-length white hair around a massive bald patch hunched over the stove. A kettle is steaming in front of him, and he picks it up to start carefully pouring the hot water into a mug.

He looks frail enough that I wonder if the sight of me will just give him a heart attack.

Two steps into the kitchen, and I'm standing behind him, my gun aimed at his head. I open my mouth to tell him calmly to turn around.

Before I can get the first word out, the hot kettle flashes toward me as he slings it over his head.

My reflexes kick in.

I dodge the hot metal, sliding to the right, but the old man grunts and tries again on the upswing. I

15

dodge backward. His brow is knit, and his eyes are cold and unfeeling. He knew I was there.

"You fucked up big time, you cock-sucker," he growls, and he seizes a knife from the counter to lunge at me.

My hand is faster.

I seize him by the wrist, and I squeeze it until I hear the snapping of bone. He gives a cry of pain, but he brings his other fist up and catches me across the face.

There's a lot more muscle behind the swing than I'd expect from someone his age.

I twist his wrist and wrench it behind his back, tired of toying with him. I kick the back of his knee and force him down over the stove, and I smell searing flesh through his scream as I press his face into the hot stovetop.

I pull him up and push him against a wall, pinning him, gun to the back of his head.

"You're no fucking fed," he growls.

"No, Geoffrey Mink," I say, my deep voice even as if my heart rate hasn't even picked up. "I am not."

"Fuck," he grunts. "You're with the mob, then? They finally come to tie off loose ends? I was like you, you know." He squirms in my grip, but he isn't going anywhere. "A hitman. One day, it'll be *your* ass on the chopping block."

"Strike two," I say with a smug smile. "I handed in my resignation to the mafia about four hours ago with the blood of the underboss and his capos in his penthouse. I'll admit, you put up a little more fight than them."

"Jesus Christ," he gasped. "I'm not a big fish, kid, I don't know why you're fucking with me. Bosses didn't tell you I'm retired?"

"Semi-retired," I corrected him, twisting his broken wrist and making him croak in pain. I feel no remorse for the monster in my grip. He was a hitman for years, but his record is blotched with innocent blood. Murdered prostitutes, sexual assault on young women who came looking for shelter, senseless violence... this man's long life is a crime against nature. "It's not you I'm interested in, Mink. It's your house."

"The fuck?"

"You've been slipping up on payments," I say. "This farmhouse was in foreclosure until I bought it three days ago. You're standing in my new safe house."

"When they find you," he says, managing a dark chuckle, "they're gonna skin you alive and feed you your own dick, kid."

I squeeze his wrist and haul him around, pushing him toward the front door. "Move. I don't want blood on my new floors."

I march him out into the cold night, out the front door and into the yard of half-frozen grass.

Snow has started to fall gently over the house. It'll be coating the ground by morning.

I force Mink to his knees, and he puts his hands behind his head as he looks down. There's a world of bitterness in this horrible old man, but even I can tell by the way his hands are shaking that he's afraid to face death after all he's done.

"How the fuck did you even find me?" he asks, his voice starting to shake.

"Did my homework," I grunt. "One of the dead men in New York was one of your last contacts. He was thinking about offering you a loan to save this house and keep you out of the way, quietly."

He lets out a rueful laugh at that. "Too little, too late. Figures." He pauses for a moment. "I think I've heard of you. Some young killer who's been making waves, and you fit the bill."

I don't answer, just staring at the back of his head down the barrel of my pistol.

"You're the one they call the Angel of Death, aren't you?" he asks, his voice barely above a hoarse whisper. I can tell by the movement of his ears that he's grinning. "I'll tell the devil you're not far behind me."

"Not without a jaw to say it," I say, and I fire the silenced shot into the back of his head, sending the bullet through the base of his skull and out his jaw. Bloody teeth hit the grass before his lifeless body follows.

The snow will have covered the blood by morning.

Slipping my gloves back on, I pick up the pieces and the corpse itself, and I start dragging it around back.

His flesh is too foul for any animals that might come sniffing at him.

I wrap him up in a tarp and find a freezer to store him in within the house for now.

My refuge.

My safe house.

I pull the car up to the place, and look it over again in a new light—not as a hunter, but as a refugee.

If I'm going to survive this winter, with the mob and cops after me, I've got a lot of work to do.

EVA

The alarm goes off at six in the morning. I sit up and stretch, then slither out of bed. The tile floor is freezing cold and I put on a pair of slippers before padding over to the kitchenette across the room. I sleepily turn on the coffee maker, rubbing my eyes.

I live in a tiny studio apartment, admittedly on the rougher side of town. It may not be much to look at, but it's mine. It's home. And I work really damn hard to maintain it.

Rent is expensive when you're on your own, and I've been on my own for a long time. I'm determined not to have a roommate, since I love coming home to peace and quiet. It's easier to focus on work when I don't have a bunch of distractions. I don't need someone around asking me questions and taking up my time. The only person who ever really looked out for me was my mother, and she's long gone now.

While the coffee is percolating, I hop into the shower and take my time washing my hair under the hot water. My apartment building is run down, a leaning, gray remnant of the seventies. The plumbing is, well, a little unreliable. Halfway through rinsing the conditioner out of my hair, the water starts to turn cold. I rush to finish up and turn it off, wrapping myself in a threadbare towel.

It's fine. I prefer them this way. I always feel like the fluffy towels don't dry as well. I quickly blow dry my long, gently curling, dark-blonde hair. I sweep it back into a bouncy ponytail and put on a little cursory makeup, just enough to make it look like I got more sleep last night than I truly did. I don't need to look perfect. I work at a daycare during the week, and the kids I look after don't care what I look like as long as I'll read to them and give them snacks.

I put on a no-nonsense green sweater and jeans, paired with some comfy boots. It's supposed to snow later today, so I throw on a thick jacket and a heavy brown scarf. Then I pour my coffee, black, into a thermos, grab my purse, and head out to catch the morning bus to work.

Today is a good day. I can tell, because on my bus ride, no weirdos sit next to me. No creepy guys leer at me and waggle their eyebrows suggestively. That's a good sign.

By the time I walk into work, I have a smile on my face. And my smile gets wider when all my favorite little kids come running up to me as I walk through the door at work.

They don't care that I live in a shitty studio in a bad neighborhood. They don't care where I come from or what my life is like. They just accept me for who I am.

And here, among the kids, I'm pretty popular. They like my singing voice that I inherited from my mom. They like the dumb knock-knock jokes I tell. They think I'm cool. Sure, it might be a little pathetic for a 23-year-old to be this happy to be liked and accepted by a bunch of kids, but whatever. I like working here. My weekdays here are a lot more fun than my weekends working at the sports bar. And my night classes for nursing school. There's a lot on my plate, but today, I feel pretty good.

I go through the whole day with a smile on my face, and when I get off work, I stop by my favorite Chinese takeout restaurant to grab some chicken lo mein for dinner. I take the bus home and to my amazement, despite the long ride and the snow, my food is still warm by the time I get to my apartment.

I settle in on the couch and watch TV while I eat. I clean up and get ready for bed. But when I walk into the curtained-off corner of the room where my bed is, suddenly it's not there.

In fact, when I look around the place, it's not my

apartment anymore. My furniture is all gone. The room isn't even the same color and shape. Now, I find myself in a dark, cold, musty room I don't recognize.

Where the hell am I?

"Help!" I cry out, and wake up with a start.

It was all a dream.

A memory replaying in my desperate mind. Just my brain trying to distract me from the horror all around me. I blink, looking around the room.

I'm not at home in my tiny but cozy studio. I'm still in this dark, gray place. I don't know where it is or how I got here. I'm in a bed, but it's not my bed. It's just the bed that exists in this room. The room I've been trapped in for what seems like days. Maybe even weeks.

My stomach churns and I rush towards the toilet, heaving over it. But there's nothing left in me to give to the porcelain god. My stomach is as empty as my soul, and my body is wracked with dry sobs.

My body aches for freedom, and I've wasted so many tears already. I haven't seen my captor since the night he first brought me down here. I've been left alone, my thoughts bleeding together, wondering how long it'll take for something to happen.

That's probably the scariest thing. That I want *something* to happen. The monotony, the fear, the sorrow, it all blends together with an aching loneliness and a pit in my heart. Every time I think I've cried my last tear and built up my resolve not to cry and scream into the nothingness anymore, I break down again.

Isn't that what he wants? To break me down?

I don't even know, because I feel broken enough already.

There are no clocks and no windows here, so I have no idea how much time has passed. I sleep almost all the time, exhausted from my tears and worries. My face feels permanently raw, my body dehydrated and losing weight, and every movement takes more energy than it ever did before. I shower to try to free myself of the grime that I feel on my skin all the time, trying to forget that I'm a captive at the whim of a mad man whose intentions I don't know.

I might as well be underground, hidden from all the world. In fact, sometimes I think I might be.

I look at the door on the other side of the room and wince at the sight of dents and scratches on the heavy industrial material. Signs of past escape attempts, when my loneliness and stir-craziness led me to beat at the door, throw things, bang canned food and the metal chair against the door, hoping desperately it might work. But nothing works. That door is solid. I don't know who built this place or who put me here, but they're got me cornered.

And under surveillance.

It only took me a little while of being here to notice the cameras. There are probably eight cameras in this small area, catching me from every angle. There's even a camera above the cracked, dusty bathroom mirror. There isn't a curtain around the bathtub, so I know my captor is trying to watch me bathe in the nude.

But I have a system: I take the sheets from my bed and drape them up over the metal rods, hiding my body as best I can. I'm not going to let this fucking scumbag win. No matter how much I scream, how much I cry, it's anger in my heart that keeps me pushing ahead. It's rage that fuels my ability to get out of the bed in the morning and not give up.

The water here is always warm. In fact, the whole place is kept at a balmy heat. It's a ploy to get me to wear less clothing, to strip down to my underwear, I just know it. But I would rather be sweaty and uncomfortable than willingly strip down and parade around half-naked for some gross pervert, wherever he is.

That's exactly what he wants, and he may have taken everything else from me, but I still have my dignity. And I intend to cling to that as long as humanly possible.

Being alone with one's thoughts is torture, especially for days or weeks on end. Especially with nothing to look forward to, no release day at the end of your stay. I can't countdown the days to my freedom. The only thing I have to look forward to is a terrifying man who kidnapped me, finally enacting the worst tortures imaginable.

I try not to think about it, pushing the dark fear into the recesses of my mind.

But in its place, all I can think about is retracing my steps of that fateful last day of freedom...

It was a normal day. Hell, even a good day. I woke up Saturday morning feeling energized and motivated. I had chores to do. Dishes to wash, laundry to fold. I blazed through all that quickly. That night I was scheduled to work the 3 o'clock to midnight shift at the sports bar. No big deal. I didn't exactly look forward to my weekend shifts there, but some nights I made pretty good money in tips. Especially if there was an important sports game happening. But I had all morning and early afternoon to myself. After I finished my chores, I decided that it was time to do something for myself. Something I had been putting off for months.

I was going to get myself a pet cat from the shelter.

Once the decision was made, I was on cloud nine. I went to the pet store and picked out all the supplies I needed. Litter box, kitty litter, cat food, scratching post, little cat toys. I was so excited.

Is that where he first saw me? I didn't recognize him at all, but if he weren't following me that night,

I'd never have given him a second glance. He just seemed so ordinary, like he would blend into any crowd.

How long had he been watching me? Was it just an impulse? Did he see me walking down the street alone and figure he got lucky?

Something tells me he was not an impulsive man, though. This horrific setup was done long in advance, the pantry stocked, the cameras put in place, the bed sheets washed. He had been planning this for a very long time.

But was he always intending it for it to be me down here in his disgusting box? Tears threaten my eyes again and I angrily swipe them away. He was no one I knew. He wasn't the parent of one of the children I look after, he wasn't a regular at the restaurant.

There was no way for you to know, I try to reassure myself, but the words ring hollow in my ears. There must have been something I could have done to prevent this.

I revisit my last day once more.

I took up so much time buying cat supplies I was almost late for work. I didn't have a chance to grab my boots to change into afterward.

I promised myself that tomorrow—Sunday—I would go to the shelter and check it out.

I'd find a sweet little kitty, maybe one that seemed neglected and afraid, and I'd nurse it back to health. I'd pour my energy into making the furball purr and feel content and safe. I was so excited.

After my shift, I was stuck walking to the bus stop in the middle of the night in my stupid work heels.

And that's when that awful man started chasing me.

He caught me.

He brought me here.

And the rest is misery.

I get up and walk around the room, wracking my brain for the thousandth time. Who could this guy be? I couldn't think of anyone who would want to cause me such harm. I was always kind of a loner, keeping to myself. Did he know that? Did he watch me and realize there was no one close to me that I could turn to?

I grew up poor, watching my mother struggle to keep us afloat. So by the time I was on my own at eighteen, I had one hell of a work ethic. I was going to tunnel my way out of poverty and make a life for myself, even if I had to isolate myself from the rest of the world to do so.

I also hated to frivolously spend money, so I always opted for public transit over taxis or ride shares. I hated working, and then spending my pay on getting to and from the restaurant. Is that why he targeted me? Did he see me on the bus one day?

I pour over my memories again, trying to piece

together his wicked grin, his hunched posture, his bulky frame.

But I'd never seen him before. Whether I saw him a hundred times in passing, or never at all, the outcome would be the same. I had no clues to go off of who this guy was.

Except for one.

He was quiet the entire time, and I was blacked out for most of it, but just before the door closed, he spoke.

"I'll be back for you when you're... ready for me," he had said before shutting and locking the bunker door, leaving my head spinning and my stomach reeling.

I still don't know what it means. When I'm ready? But I have the worst feeling about it. That he wants to break me down. That he wants me to go to those cameras and beg for him to rescue me from this Hell on Earth. That he wants me broken and simpering, desperate for any kind of human touch.

Even his.

My stomach growls and my face twists in anger. Every time I have to do anything other than sleep, I feel like my body is betraying me. Acting like everything is normal, and this isn't the worst thing to happen to me.

How can I worry about hunger, about showering, about doing *anything* when I'm just a toy to an absent kidnapper?

But he's never really absent. I walk over to the little kitchenette area and stare up at the hidden camera with anger and hate in my eyes. It's a dark kind of poetry how similar this place is to my studio apartment. Same small square footage. Same stark, minimalistic decor.

Except my apartment was my sanctuary, filled with my treasured possessions, and allowing me to come and go as I needed. I had my freedom. My privacy.

My sanity.

This place is like a hellish shadow of my apartment.

Whoever put me here had the place fully stocked, though. There were plenty of towels and rolls of toilet paper. The kitchenette had a massive pantry filled with canned goods and preserved food. None of it was particularly tasty, but my captor wasn't starving me.

If he wants me begging for him, it's probably just another ploy to try to get me on his side. His own twisted version of bad cop, good cop, but he's both players.

I try to remember more from that day when I was brought here. After that man chased me into the alleyway, I fell. I cut my foot. It still hurts, even now, after washing it profusely and keeping it clean. It doesn't look infected, and I've stayed off it as best I can. What else is there to do?

After I fell down, the man caught me. I tried to slash at him with a piece of glass but I couldn't do it. There was that nasty sweet smell and then I blacked out. I assume he chloroformed me. I remember little bits and pieces, vaguely. Waking up in a moving vehicle, lying on my back. I couldn't move or speak for some reason. I saw flashes of moonlight through the trees. And then nothing, until I woke up here, in this room.

"I'll be back for you when you're... ready for me."

The last words I've heard spoken to me in days. Weeks maybe.

There is something else I remember, but it has nothing to do with why I'm here. There's no way it could. A few weeks ago, someone I had no memory of, no attachment to, decided to suddenly appear. Someone I never expected to see. Someone I didn't even miss.

My father.

In between my tears, my anger, my fear, I keep mulling over the strange details of our meetup. It's a distraction from my horrific situation, but not a very pleasant one.

The man who ignored my existence for twenty-three years, this complete stranger who wanted nothing to do with me or my mother, suddenly wanted to see me. When I walked into his office at the manufacturing plant he owns in Rochester, he looked ill. Tired. He was pale and fragile-looking, nothing like the strong man I used to imagine when I was a child.

I was suspicious of his intentions. After all, what could he possibly have wanted with me now after all this time? But it seemed to me he was feeling guilty. Ashamed, maybe, of how he treated mom and I.

Like he wanted to make up for lost time or something.

"Too late for that," I frown morosely, feeling my stomach growl again and ignoring it.

My biological father mentioned something about a will, some paperwork he decided to add my name to. But I knew not to get excited about that. All my life, he has let me down. Pretended I don't exist. Why should I expect anything from him now?

Besides, I don't want anything from him. I prefer to make my own way in life. I don't want to owe anything to anyone.

And now it doesn't matter anyway. Because I'm trapped down here in this horrible pit, being watched and stalked by some creepy old pervert.

"Sorry, Dad. I've already got one awful old man trying to ruin my life right now, don't have room for another," I mumble.

I walk to my bed, slowly stripping the sheets once more. It's the only real routine I have, something I can turn my brain off on. Just go through the motions of taking the sheets, hanging them on the metal shower rod. Everything in here is damp from the humidity of my constant showers, but I can't help but feel like I'm coated in something nasty.

Especially knowing that the cameras are tracking my every move.

I turn on the water, the warm steam filling the air. If I close my eyes, for just a second, I can pretend I'm back in my own apartment, showering in the morning to get ready for the day. I imagine the hands of daycare kids wrapping me in a hug, tickling me and brightening my day. I can almost smell the scent of tempra paint and the outdoors and their lunches in my nose, and a faint smile reluctantly comes to my lips.

But I'm not there, and my breath gets choked off in my throat. A sob comes from me, and in the only private place I have, I begin to truly cry. Not to anguished, angry and frighten cries of earlier in my captivity.

These are the tears of grief. Of mourning.

As if I'd finally accepted that my old life is dead and gone, and all I have to look forward to is up to the whims of a disgusting creep.

Tears mingle with the shower water and my shoulders heave until there's no more tears to cry. I'm empty, the sensation almost cathartic after feeling so much for so long. I stay in the shower until it runs cold, wanting to hide my vulnerability from those damnable cameras. I don't want him to know he's won. That he's beaten me down.

"I'll be back for you when you're ready for me," he promised. I never want him to think I'm ready for him. I'll *never* be ready for him.

I reach for the towel, drawing it in behind the sheet, drying off quickly, my body starting to shiver from the cold water. My clothes don't smell so nice anymore, after being down here for so long, but I grab for them and discreetly get dressed in the tub.

In the corner of the room is a dresser with brand new lacy lingerie and other pieces of scant clothing. I won't wear any of it. As I walk out of the bathroom I turn and flip the mirror camera the bird. I mouth the words *fuck you.* I'm not going to let him know he won.

But even with all my anger and fear, I find myself torn. I certainly don't want that nasty old pervert to come down here. I never want to see his horrible fucking face again.

On the other hand, being alone with my thoughts for so long... I'm losing my grip on reality. Loneliness eats at me, and not knowing what's going to happen, imagining every horrific possibility... At least if he came down here, I'd know more of what to expect. At least I'd have something solid to fear.

I'm pushed from my reverie by the sound at the door.

I freeze up, looking over at the door with wide eyes. My heart begins to pound.

No, no, no no no!

I immediately move to the kitchen, looking for a weapon. There's no knives, and the sharpest thing in there is a can opener. I grab a can of tomato soup, hoping I could throw it at him and dart for the door.

Now that he's here, I definitely know what I want. I want to be free. I want the third option.

I can hear a series of locks clicking, coming undone. And then the door knob turns. The door clicks open and a beam of light pours into the room, illuminating the dark silhouette in the doorway.

Instantly I can tell that it's not the same man. This man is broad and very tall, blocking off the entire door with his wall of muscle. I gulp and reel the can back, preparing to throw it at his head as I shake with fear.

"Who the hell are you?"

SALVATORE

*A*nger flashes behind my eyes, but when I see Mink's secret in the flesh, I'm stunned into silence.

A woman. The most beautiful woman I've ever seen.

Her face hits me like lightning. She has icy blue eyes that shine brighter than anything else in the furnished room around her. Her dark blonde hair is long, past her shoulders, and even in the bad lighting, it seems to shine like a golden halo.

She's a full foot shorter than me, and I recognize the look on her face. I know the sight of it well.

Fear.

We're both frozen in place for a long moment, stunned at each other. Her eyes look me up and down. I'm wearing a tight black tank top and my usual black jeans. I loom in the doorway, my breathing heavy and my jaw tightening.

Until this morning, I thought the shed behind the house was just some storage space for old junk. I couldn't have been more surprised when I stepped inside.

It was a surveillance room.

There were computers, camera setups, and video feeds all over the interior. It looked like a security guard's room.

I saw what I thought was a recording of a girl walking around on the screens. I assumed it was some strange fetish porn the old man liked to watch.

Then I found the hatch in the floor.

When I opened the thing up, I felt like I'd found a staircase to the underworld. It was a long staircase into darkness, and the light bulb I turned on flickered and revealed cobwebs most of the way down.

Then a military grade door, keeping whatever was locked inside a secret from the outside world. Mink had kept his secret well, and no one would have been able to find her should he have lived. He was careful, and in the middle of nowhere, surrounded by concrete and steel, no one would have heard her scream for help.

She was his prisoner, but I have no idea for how long. Pity swarms my heart, and it brings a bitter taste to my mouth. I shove it all down, anger rising up in me once more.

I have a living, breathing problem on my hands. One I can't simply murder and run away from. I might be the *Angel of Death*, but I do not kill children or women. That was one of the reasons why all my mafia contacts are dancing with the Devil, now.

So what can I do with a lovely, broken captive that I've inherited?

I take a few steps into the room, and as soon as I do, she starts running toward me at full tilt. I'm taken by surprise, and she tries to run past me out the door, scrambling like a wild animal.

I catch her around the waist and pull her back. Immediately, she starts kicking and scratching at me, a can of tomato soup smashing against my bicep before slipping from her hands and denting on impact. She doesn't try to lunge for it, instead battering her little fists off my rippling muscles like rain as I hold her back and grip her wrists as she struggles.

I don't want to hurt her, but she's going to hurt herself like this.

"Get the fuck off me, let me go!" she cries, thrashing in my arms.

"Calm down," I grunt, "I'm not going to hurt—"

"Fuck off!" she shouts, trying to lean around me and shout, "Help! Help!" up the stairs.

"I'm not going to hurt you!" I say in a firm, commanding voice as I pull her off me and pin her arms to her side, holding her away from me and looking into her terrified face. "Listen to me. What are you doing down here?"

She breathes heavily a few seconds, watching me with wild eyes as her chest rises and falls, color flush in her cheeks.

Her gaze goes to my hands, then to my chest. The anger in her face starts to fade, and it slowly gives way to something else. Something I'm more used to seeing when people look at me.

Fear.

"You're... you're not him," she says at last, more to herself than to me.

"No. I'm not *him*."

"Your grip is different. You're way too big," she says, talking to herself. "And the smell, too. You're not him. Are you... did that bastard send you to kill me?"

"No. I'm not here to kill you."

I look her in the eye, and I see a hundred emotions in that intense expression. She's anxious, terrified, confused, and still a little angry, but there's something else in that gaze.

How long has it been since she's seen another person? Longing lingers beneath her heavy lashes, and that's confusing to me. Concerning. But perhaps I can use that to my advantage. If she's been down here this long, if she's desperate for anyone but Mink to visit her...

"Let me prove that I'm not here to hurt you. I'm

going to let you go. Do not try to run. I'm not him, but you're still in the middle of nowhere with me, and the quicker we can work this out, the better it will be for both of us."

She looks up at me with defiance at first, but I can see the conflict in her eyes. There's desperation there, too.

Finally, she relents, and I release her arms, my eyes narrowing critically at her.

She rubs her arms and immediately backs away from me and moves to her bed. It's a rickety-looking thing, but the way she moves to it makes it seem like it's the one thing in the room that brings her any comfort. She sits down on it, her posture closing up, and her hands grab handfuls of her blanket.

My eyes move from it to the bathroom area. There are no walls, and the shower has no curtain. I clench my jaw, thinking back to all the camera feeds set up in the room above us. All of them showed a room... this room.

Mink was watching her every move.

She was his sick little perverted game.

"What are you doing here? Do you work for him?" she asks, her voice still suspicious, but her eyes keep moving up and down me.

"No," I say simply, taking another step into the room. "Who's this 'him' you keep talking about?" I already know, of course, but if Mink had friends, or someone else who knew of this woman, things could get messy very quickly.

"I... I don't know," she says, her lip quivering. "The guy who put me here."

I think carefully about how to approach this. Judging by this woman's mental state, she has probably been down here a while. I've met soldiers of the mafia who have spent long spans of time in solitary confinement with no other human contact.

It can have serious effects on their psyches. And those were hardened criminals, men who knew why they were in solitary. She's desperate for answers, and very fragile. She didn't have the training those men had, didn't have the constitution.

I take another step into the room. She watches me carefully, but she doesn't move.

"Do you know how long you've been down here?"

She seems to try to think for a moment, but she swallows and shakes her head. "There are no windows and no clocks." Her eyes are rimmed with tears. "It... it feels like a lifetime."

"You said someone put you here," I say. "Were you taken against your will?"

"Do I look like I want to be here?" she snaps, but she immediately softens, and I see tears roll down her cheeks as she buries her face in her hands, sobbing.

I stiffen, watching her, unsure what to do. I

haven't had contact with another person since killing the previous owner, and I'd never been one for the company of others. Especially when they were... vulnerable.

For a brief second, I think back to a brief moment in my past, the last time I saw a woman cry. I was only a child then, but it was in that second I knew that women were special. Something to be protected and guarded against the hurt in the world.

And then I became the hurt in the world.

Is this a chance to make amends for all the hearts I broke? All the husbands and fathers I took from the world?

Slowly, I walk toward her, and once I'm close enough to her bed, I kneel down in front of her to look at her on her level. She gasps in surprise when she realizes how quickly and quietly I approached her, and she recoils a little, but she doesn't run.

She just stares at me with those wet, blue eyes.

She probably still thinks this is some kind of dream. Some horrible, hopeful fever dream.

"Do you want to come out of here?" I ask her, trying to keep my gravelly voice soft.

It seems like a question with an obvious answer, but one glance around the room says so much. There are signs of her living in it everywhere. With no human contact, no view of the outside world, this place *has* been her whole world for god knows how long.

She looks at me with foggy eyes, as if I'd just spoken a foreign language to her.

I hold out my hand to her, and she stares at it for a few moments before carefully putting her small hand in my palm.

She seems almost surprised that my hand feels real. Despite everything, she feels warm and soft.

I close my hand around hers and stand up slowly.

"I don't even know where I am," she breathes, her voice so delicate.

"Let me show you," I say. "Trust me for a moment."

After a pause, she nods.

I take a few slow steps backward until we reach the threshold of the door. She looks at it cautiously, as if wondering if this is a trap.

Finally, she walks over it with me, and she squints up at the stairway to the exit before I gently guide her up.

As we climb the stairs carefully, one thought haunts my mind.

Who is this angel I've found down here in the bowels of hell? And what am I going to do with her now that she's seen my face?

EVA

*J*step up into the yellowish light of the shed, my heart thumping like crazy. As I look around the room, my mouth falls open and I can feel tears burning in my eyes.

But I'm not crying because I'm finally free from that fucking bunker.

I'm crying because this room is a pervert's paradise.

There have got to be ten or eleven different monitors around the room, and every screen shows a different angle of the bunker I was being held inside. It's even worse than I thought. When I was trapped, I assumed that the blinking camera over the mirror was the only bathroom camera. But I was wrong. There are three different angles of the bathroom, one of which is more or less inside the shower. Which tells me that even when I draped a bed sheet over the metal shower rod to form a makeshift courtesy curtain, it didn't matter. There was an even more intimately-placed camera watching me the whole time.

Watching me naked in the shower, washing my body.

There was a camera staring down over the top of my bed and another that had to have been somehow affixed to the headboard. So that creep could watch me sleep from an aerial view as well as an up close and personal view. Hell, he could probably watch me drool in my sleep, could hear every snore, every shudder, every time I cried under the sheets wishing someone would come and rescue me.

There's a camera implanted somewhere inside the door, too. The view faces out from the doorway, pointed slightly downward. That means that every time I scratched and slammed and screamed at the door, he was watching me. Closely. Close enough to see the terror in my eyes, the tears rolling hot down my cheeks. This is more than just some sexual fantasy, this is the lair of a sadistic predator who got off on watching me suffer. It dawns on me that he was probably intending to keep me there forever, just eating popcorn while he watched me descend into insanity and hopelessness.

I crumple to the floor, my knees buckling beneath me as I bury my face in my hands.

My savior, if he really is saving me, crouches

down beside me and puts an arm over my back. But I don't want to be touched right now. Not while I'm feeling so exposed and vulnerable. I shrug away from him, sobbing. To his credit, he backs away, listening to my body language.

"I'm sorry," he says in that low, rough voice. There is genuine sorrow in his tone, and while I appreciate the concern, it also just makes me angry. I don't want to be pitied. I don't want this complete stranger's first impression of me to be that I'm weak and fragile. No. I won't let myself be broken. At least, I don't want him to see me that way, even if I am.

And at this point, surrounded by all these surveillance monitors, I *am* broken. And alone. All alone and confused and shattered. I look up from my hands at the man who freed me. Tall, powerful, dressed in black with a somber expression on his impossibly handsome face. There's a gentleness, a quiet, restrained power that intrigues me even more than it frightens me.

Before I can think twice about it, I get up and dash into his arms, burying my face into his shoulder. He freezes up for a second, clearly surprised at my sudden change of heart. But then he holds me, his hands patting my back, cradling me like a wounded animal against his chest.

I wish I wasn't doing this. I wish I wasn't so weak. I'm stronger than this, or at least I thought I was. But something about this man makes me feel safe.

Or maybe it's just the loneliness, the absence of human touch for so long. I never realized how much the hugs from the kids, the brushing of hands as a customer handed me a tip, the way my shoulders pressed against someone else on the bus could be missed. I always considered myself a loner, but those little social interactions... I missed them more than I can put into words.

"He was watching me," I murmur into his black shirt, damp from my tears. "All that time, he was watching me. I knew he was. But…"

"You didn't know how closely," he finishes for me in a solemn voice.

I nod, my shoulders shaking with sobs. "I-I didn't know. That whole time, there was nowhere to hide."

"How long have you been down there?" he asks again, stroking my hair. I push back and look at his face, searching for the answer myself.

"I don't know. There are no clocks. No windows. I-I just slept when I was tired. There was no way to keep track of time," I admit, shrugging helplessly.

He frowns, his jaw tightening.

"What is your name?"

I blink a few times, confused at the change of subject. At first, I worry that I should keep my identity secret, just in case this guy is actually working with my captor. But that thought quickly vanishes.

The man that put me in that hole would never let another person see me, or speak to me. The cameras tell me that much. He wanted to control me, utterly.

For perhaps the first time, I believe he truly is my rescuer, and not just someone toying with me.

So I tell him the truth.

"My name is Eva. Eva Wells," I say, sniffling.

"Okay, Eva," he says, and the sound of his deep voice growling my name sends a shiver down my spine. "Do you know what year it is?"

"It's 2017," I tell him, frowning. Why is he asking me this?

He looks relieved. "Good, good. What month?"

I bite my lip. "December?"

The hint of a smile plays on his lips. "That's right. And what is the last date you can remember for certain? Do you remember the date of the day you were brought here?"

I close my eyes and think about it for a moment. "It was a Saturday. I had just gotten off work. It was... the ninth?"

The man winces, which tells me that's not good, somehow. "What? What does that mean?" I ask frantically. He puts a hand on my shoulder, calming me.

"It just means you've been down there for a while. A few weeks. Have you been eating? There's food down there? Or has he... has he been feeding you?" he asks.

I shudder. "There are cans of food. Peas and

carrots and tuna. Stuff like that. I never saw him. Once he threw me in there, he never came in. Not to my knowledge," I add, wondering darkly if maybe that pervert had ever come into my room while I was sleeping or something. After seeing all these monitors, I wouldn't put it past him.

"Are you hungry?"

"Yeah. Starving."

"Okay. Let's get to the main building, then," he says, leading me out of the shed into the light of morning. I thought it was late afternoon, supposed to be almost dark. Weeks in that bunker...

"The sun," I mumble. It hurts, but it's a hurt I crave right now, after all that time down there.

"Still shining," says my savior.

He leads me across a big, overgrown yard and into a different building. It looks like an old farm-house, badly dilapidated in some places and still mostly upright in others. It looks like the kind of place a squatter might take up residence, and I wonder if maybe my captor was squatting here ille-gally. I had no idea any of this was here, no reason to suspect there was anything above ground. All I knew was the bunker.

We walk into a kitchen, which is surprisingly well-maintained. Even clean.

"How long have you been here?" I ask suddenly, looking around.

He doesn't answer.

"Do you like grilled cheese sandwiches?" he says.

My stomach growls.

"I'll eat anything that doesn't come from a can," I say plainly, taking a seat at the little table in the middle of the kitchen while he takes out a pan, bread, butter, and a block of cheddar cheese. I watch him as he cooks, seeing the muscles ripple across his powerful back.

"How long have you been here?" I ask again. "The kitchen looks clean. Different from the rest of the house."

Without turning around, he answers, "A few days. I'm restoring the place. Starting with the kitchen."

"So, what are you? A construction guy?" I ask. He snorts. "Cop?" I suggest.

He glances back at me, one eyebrow raised. I roll my eyes.

"Okay, not a cop, either. I guess that makes sense. A cop wouldn't be making me a sandwich. He would just take me straight to the police station to take a statement."

He stops and turns around, folding his arms over his chest.

"Do you want to go to the police station?" he asks, his tone tense. He doesn't want me to say yes.

And surprisingly, I don't want to say yes. I don't want to go.

Not now.

Not yet.

Maybe not ever.

I don't want anyone to know what happened to me. Shame burns in my face as I think of all the things people would say. All the things they've said to me and countless others before. That I shouldn't have taken the bus so late, that I should have walked with a male escort, that I should've been more careful, that I shouldn't have been wearing heels.

I don't want to face that scrutiny.

It makes me dizzy, all the self-blame from the last several weeks, ever since I'd been captured, swirling in my mind. But deep down, I know it wasn't my fault.

No one wants to be held captive in a bunker. No one could do anything to deserve that fate, or ask for that fate.

"No," I answer quietly, breaking myself out of my reverie.

"Good," he says, turning back to the grilled cheese in the pan.

I get up and walk over to stand beside him.

"Why? Why is that good?"

He's silent for a long time. Then he says simply, "It's not safe for you to leave."

"Why?" I press on. He gives me a silencing look and I close my mouth.

I stare at him, the gears churning in my mind. I

know he's hiding something from me. A lot of some-things, I imagine.

But he is the man who saved me from hell, and I find myself drawn to him. He's tall, and strong, and hasn't done anything to make me think he wants to hurt me. I lick my lips, pondering things over.

He's a stranger. I shouldn't trust just anyone.

So why do I already trust him? Why do I believe him when he says it's not safe for me to leave?

"Your sandwich is done," he says, pulling me from my thoughts as he flips the grilled cheese onto a plate and hands it to me. The bread is the perfect brown color, the cheese melted just outside of the crust, and pulling apart into a beautiful, gooey, wholesome half.

Comfort food, I think to myself, savoring the flavor of something fresh and delicious. I never knew how much I missed bread. A sensual moan escapes my lips, and I cover my mouth, embarrassed. I feel his gaze on me, a slight smile brightening his otherwise serious face.

Something lingers in his gaze. Almost like...

Gratitude?

No. I must be mistaken. But the longer he watches me, the more I stare at him, the more I get a glimpse into his soul. Into the loneliness we share. The gratitude of just having someone else, some other calming presence in the room.

I dab my lip with a napkin, and I smile back at

him. His face softens at me, and my heart pounds faster in my chest. All the while I was in the bunker, I was terrified I'd never see anyone else's face but for the kidnapper.

But now, I'm looking at a rugged, handsome man, who seems smitten with my enjoyment of the food he made me. The moment only lasts a second before he seems to realize how intensely our eyes are locked and he turns away, heading into another room.

I stare after him, confused. A few moment later I hear the sounds of metal and plastic clinking together, like he's rummaging through a drawer. I get up, taking my sandwich with me, and walk into what appears to be a living room.

"What are you doing?" I ask.

He holds up a toolbox. "Restoration."

"Now?" I ask, half annoyed and half amused.

"No time like the present."

"So, freeing a trapped captive woman from a bunker is just another item on your to-do list and now you've moved on to... whatever it is you're doing there?" I comment, taking a big bite of my sandwich.

He shrugs.

"I suppose so."

He's trying to seem normal, like this is nothing, but I can see the gears churning behind his eyes. He doesn't know what to do with me, and he's trying to figure it out. Figure me out. Perhaps that's why he wanted the silent routine of hammering.

I sit down on the musty sofa while he lays out tools on the coffee table. Wrenches, hammers, screws. He means business.

I don't want him to figure out what to do with me. Not yet. For now, I just want to sit here, and savor my freedom.

There's a darker part of me, though. A darker part of me that was lost in fantasies in the bunker, doing everything I could to escape that hellhole. I tried in vain so many times to physically escape, so instead I used to dream about what would happen after I left. I thought about my lonely, quiet existence before the bunker. No boyfriends, no friends, no family but for an absentee father.

All I could dream about was changing that. Finding someone who would always protect me. Someone who would be looking for me if I went missing. Someone who would save me, time and time again.

I don't know if God heard my prayers or not, but either way, the universe sent me a savior, and I don't intend to run away from fate.

"What's your name?" I ask.

"Salvatore. Sal," he adds with a bit of softness as he gets up to walk into another room, hammer in hand.

I follow after him.

Over the course of the day, I continue to follow him, afraid to let him out of my sight for even a moment. I ask him question after question. Sometimes he answers. Sometimes he doesn't. But he never loses patience, answering me with the same calmness. It reminds me of how I'd answer the questions at the daycare, though without the excitement and happiness.

There is a part of me that wants to leave, to bust out of this house and just run. Run in whatever direction, running back to the life I'd built for myself. It's not too late. My job might be gone, but my rent hasn't even come due yet. I could slide back into the routine of my old life.

But after weeks in the bunker, hidden from the world, I feel like something fundamental inside me has snapped. Can I ever return to normal?

No. Not so soon, at least. I'm terrified of being alone, and I crave the company of someone who understands what I went through without me having to say anything more. My tight-lipped savior. The only one who I'll never need to explain what happened to me to.

Besides, I don't trust myself to survive on my own. I don't know how far we are from Rochester, or if we're even in the same state anymore. I know nothing, and Sal is the closest thing to an answer I have.

He saved me. He makes me feel solid and stable

for the first time in weeks. I don't want to leave him. Right now, I'm just reveling in the freedom of getting to walk around a house above ground, safe in the knowledge that some pervert isn't holed up watching me on a bunch of monitors anymore.

I'm relieved. So relieved that I don't even get angry when Sal doesn't answer a question. Maybe he's just like me—keeping to himself. Maybe the world has hurt him somehow, too. Maybe he doesn't trust me.

So why do I trust him?

"If you've been here three days, how did you just now find me?" I ask.

"I assumed the shed was in disrepair like the rest of the property. I figured it'd just be a broken down mower in it, but hoped to find some paint in there," he explains.

"Why are you here?" I inquire.

"I've told you a thousand times. To restore the property."

"What happened to that man who brought me here?"

"Don't worry about him."

"How do I not worry about him? He's a crazy sadist who locked me in a bunker to watch my every move for nearly a month!"

Sal gives me a stern expression, anger and something else swirling in his cool gaze.

"He's not a problem anymore."

"Why not?"

"He has been dealt with."

"How? Where did he go? What if he comes back?"

Sal sighs, looking down at his watch.

"It's seven PM. Do you want dinner?"

I stop short, again diverted by food. Turns out, living on dusty old canned food for weeks does wonders for your appetite. Sal cooks us a steak split between the two of us, and couple of baked potatoes with cheese and sour cream, the likes of which I had assumed I would never taste again. After dinner, I immediately start to feel sleepy, my internal clock totally warped from my time without clocks or sunlight.

"You should rest," he says.

"Where?" I ask, my eyes feeling heavy.

"The kitchen is the cleanest room, but there's a bedroom you can use. I'll show you," he says, beckoning for me to follow him. I trudge behind him across the house to a Spartan bedroom. The dresser and bedside table are coated in a layer of dust, but the bed looks reasonable enough.

"The sheets have been cleaned," he says. "I've been using the bed while I stay here."

"Where will you sleep then?" I ask, turning to look at him with concern.

"Don't worry about me. I'll be fine," he says.

"No, that's not fair to you," I protest. There's a look of faint surprise on his face, like he's confused that I would worry about where he's sleeping tonight. I get the feeling he's not used to anyone worrying about him, in general.

"I will be fine. There's another bedroom. And a couch," he explains. Before he turns away, he adds, "How long have you been wearing those clothes?"

I look down at my outfit. The same one I wore the day I was captured. I can't help but blush. They must look and smell a little off. "A while," I answer sheepishly.

"Do you want something of mine to wear instead?" he asks.

I bite my lip, considering the awkwardness of wearing this man's clothing. He's gigantic, and I'm five-foot-six and slender. But it beats wearing this stupid sports bar uniform.

"Yes, please," I admit. He nods and walks away, leaving me alone in the room for a few minutes. During those minutes, my panic returns and my heart races. It's like the second he's out of my sight, the terror returns. Like he's the only thing keeping me tethered to reality.

I sit on the bed, the blankets wrapped around me as I just try to breathe through the panic attack, tears coming to my eyes as I angrily swat them away.

"You're not down there anymore," I say to myself, trying to reassure my fractured mind. My lip trembles as I shake my head. "This is normal. It's normal to be scared," I say out loud. "But I'm safe now."

He comes back holding a pair of boxer shorts and a huge white T-shirt, looking at me curiously. In the few minutes it's been since he left, I must look like a totally different person. Panic stricken, curled up on the bed in terror, talking to myself.

But he doesn't force me to explain myself, his rough voice still tender with me.

"I apologize for the boxers, but somehow I don't think I have any pants that would fit you," he says, with just a tiny hint of humor.

I wipe my face again and gratefully take the clothes. They smell like a combination of laundry detergent and... Sal.

"Well, I'll leave you to it," he says. "If you need anything, just come find me."

"Sal?" I pipe up as he walks away. He looks back at me. I blush. "You aren't going to... you won't..."

"Leave?" he fills in. I nod. "No. I'm not going anywhere, Eva."

"Thank you," I murmur, tears prickling in my eyes again.

"Good night, Eva," he says softly. As he walks out of the room, it's like all the light disappears from the world. My heart is heavy. That old fear is creeping back in. But this time, I cling to his clothes, smelling him on my body as I change.

The scent shouldn't be so reassuring, but it is. It's fresh, and masculine, and brings up such strange feelings to me. It's enough to comfort my panic, and make me feel safe.

Tomorrow, I promise myself. Tomorrow, I'll figure it all out. But for now I need to sleep. I need this so badly. Before my head even hits the pillow, my eyes draw closed, and sleep claims me. I find myself back in my old bed, my little studio apartment that I've longed for during these long weeks.

It smells like home.

But it also smells like Sal. Just like that, he appears, his eyes sparkling as he looks at me, his mouth moving against the hollow of my neck. It's a place that's never been explored, and my entire body feels electric.

I moan, my fingers going through his hair, my body starting to writhe against his in explicit pleasure. "Sal," I whimper to him, and he looks at me with such affection.

But then his expression goes serious.

"I dealt with your captor. And now I have to deal with you," he says as his face shifts and twists, becoming that shadowy smile of my kidnapper.

I awake with a start, biting down on my hand to silence my scream of terror.

It all comes back to me, the dream mixing with reality in such a horrifying way.

Sal said the guy who brought me here was "dealt with." What the hell does that mean? *Dealt with* how? Was he arrested? Run off the property?

Killed?

For all I know, he killed my captor, in cold blood.

Who the hell is Sal?

He saved me. That's for certain. But why? If he killed my captor so easily, what is there to keep him from doing the same to me?

Is my savior a murderer?

And was my dream trying to tell me what I already know, but refuse to admit to myself?

SALVATORE

I get up before dawn, my eyes opening into the darkness as if I'd never slept.

I've been a light sleeper all my life, but my job kept me from ever falling into a deep sleep. Last night was more tense than usual, listening for every creak of the house.

If Eva escapes, if she tells anyone what she's found here, then I'm going to have a lot more attention than I need. Cops will be the least of my problems. Once the mafia finds out my location, they will send every freelance hitman my way, wanting me to pay for my sins.

But the night was silent, nothing but the sounds of the woods.

Silent footsteps carry me to my wardrobe, where I dress warmly: a sweater under a heavy jacket, a simple gray scarf, gloves, and sunglasses. It helps me stay anonymous as well as warm.

I head to the kitchen and pour myself a cup of coffee to wake myself up, but as I try to drink it quickly, I hear the creak of a floorboard behind me. I don't turn around, because I know she's there, her sky-blue eyes watching me curiously.

"You're leaving," she points out. Without turning my gaze from the window, I nod. There's a pause as she stares at me before speaking again. "Can I come with you?"

I shake my head.

"Why not?"

I don't respond at first. With another swig of the steaming coffee, I finish it and set the mug down before I turn to face her.

"Not safe," I say simply as my dark eyes meet her form. Even in the dim light of the kitchen, she seems to glow, her blonde hair and blue eyes making her stand out like an angel. Her hair is tied back in a messy ponytail, and she looks tiny in my oversized shirt and boxers, knees together and hands wringing the edge of the shirt.

She looks scared already.

"Please," she says, daring to take a step closer to me. "I-I've been alone for almost a month, I just want someone to be able to talk to. I won't be a bother."

I give her a long, stern stare.

"It's not safe," I repeat more slowly, like that will help her to understand the seriousness of my words. Her face falls. I've grown hard to the sadness of others over the years, but her face makes even me feel a twinge of guilt at twisting the knife into her.

She struggles to find words, any words that could change my mind, but she just opens and closes her mouth a few times, failing. Instead, she just looks at me desperately. I draw in a deep breath and let it out slowly, striding over to her and looking down at her sleepy face.

"I won't be long," I say simply. "We need supplies. Food for two." I reach to her shoulder and pluck the shirt hanging on her shoulders. "And clothes."

"Shouldn't I come pick some out? You don't even know my size," she says, a feeble smile on her face. I have to give her credit for trying.

"I do."

Her eyelashes flutter.

"Wait, what? How?"

"I'm a good judge," I say, and I move past her, taking the keys out of my pocket. As I open the door, I turn and give her a meaningful look. "Stay inside."

"What if I don't?" she asks, the shadow of a pout in her tone. I stare at her long and hard, and she seems to shrink back.

"Then I cannot protect you."

She opens her mouth to protest, but my look silences her, and she nods.

I shut the door behind me and lock it, pulling my jacket tighter around me to blunt the sting of the cold winter air. This one has been especially brutal.

I can't encourage her need to be around me. I'm not the type of man she needs to be around right now. But neither of us have a choice. She might feel free, but she's just as trapped as she was beneath the bunker, she just doesn't realize it.

True freedom, for her, would leave us both buried in an unmarked grave, or tossed into the freezing cold Atlantic Ocean.

And I wasn't lying when I said it would be too dangerous for her this morning.

It was true that I needed to make a supply run. I got into my car and pulled out of the driveway, winding through the wintery morning and out onto the road toward Rochester.

My list included construction materials for the renovations on the house as well as enough food and clothes to take care of her. I'm a man with simple needs: I can live on rice and beans for a long time. But she's spent the past few weeks locked away with nothing but the bland canned food the wretched old man left for her.

I still don't know what I'm going to do with her. For now, I'm going to see to it that she's well fed and feeling... safe, before I decide. Right now, she can't leave. I have a little house of cards, and she could easily blow them all down.

She's my captive. She just doesn't know it yet. To her, I'm the man who saved her from a far worse fate. But while her kidnapper was evil, even he doesn't have the blood on his hands that I do. And when she eventually pieces it together, what happened to him...

No women. No kids. Those are my laws, the only laws I've ever listened to.

But I've never had a problem with a woman like this one. I once heard a saying that when you think like a hammer, every problem looks like a nail. A gun and a bullet has always been my weapon of choice, but the saying remains true.

And those options are off the table.

So what do I do with the beautiful woman who tentatively trusts me? Who longs to be around me, until she finds out my truth and decides to turn me in when she runs to the cops?

She can never know the truth.

I let out a heavy sigh, staring at the road ahead. White all around me tries to dull my senses, but my mind is a hive of activity, and my eyes remain sharp as I mull over my options.

The sky ahead of me starts to turn purple as I drive, and along the side of the road, I see deer running away from the sound of my engine as I roar down the roads. I've never been much of a country person, but since being out here, I've come to appreciate the sights and sounds of nature before the world has woken up.

My eyes scan the roads to my sides as I roll through Rochester's streets before the morning traffic has started in earnest. The fewer people that see me, the better.

I wonder how things have been going down in New York City since I did what I did. There is no other way to describe my situation—I am in hiding, laying low, and I haven't had any contact with any of my old associates since I massacred my old bosses.

There are even some who might be sympathetic to what I did, but even if I could trust another soul, there is nobody I know well enough that I'd reach out to them. I've been a lone wolf most of my time in the mafia.

Hitmen often work alone, and my reputation keeps most at an arm's length.

I expected to spend the next few *years* alone, in hiding. Perhaps longer.

That made discovering Eva all the more difficult.

As I pull up to the supermarket that's open twenty-four hours, I think about the sight of her standing there in the doorway this morning.

What am I to make of this strange, broken girl?

She's desperate, but she hasn't made an attempt to run away yet. Is she hiding from something? Does she expect something from me? Perhaps my new captive isn't as innocent as she seems.

Her eyes search me every time they look at me. I know that look from the people I'm about to kill, that searching gaze that tries to look into my soul.

She doesn't know what to make of me, and I don't know what to do with her. It's a suiting enough scenario, but I can't help but feel heavy in my heart as I consider my options.

Soldiers of the mafia who have spent time in solitary confinement say that even three days in a place like that feels like a month. No contact, just four walls and the loneliness of your thoughts.

It is impressive that this young woman is not completely broken. But her resilience could be a thorn in my side.

I get a variety of basics from the store. Pasta, canned tomatoes and sauce, rice, some spices, beef and pork that I can freeze and work with, some eggs, and plenty of canned vegetables. As I go by the cheeses in the deli, I pause thoughtfully. I've never been a man who cares much for luxury, but after a particularly hard job, I would sometimes enjoy the evening with cheese and good wine.

So, I add a wheel of brie, a block of manchego, and a slab of parmesan to my cart and grab a bottle of decent red wine before I move on to the clothes section of the store.

As soon as I get there, I frown, realizing I have no idea how to shop for a woman like her.

But I will have to keep her at the house for some

time, so I decide a little bit of everything useful will have to do. All she had on her was the clothes she was captured in, with the little logo of some bar above the left breast. The only other clothes I found in the bunker were new lingerie that hadn't looked touched, let alone put on. He was trying to wear her down into being his sex doll, and the thought makes me sneer.

I wish I'd known what he was doing when I killed him, so I could truly make that sick fuck suffer. If I could, I'd kill him all over again, this time as slow as he deserved. The fantasy of stuffing him, bleeding, in that bunker...

My pulse quickened, and a twisted smile came to my lips. I push the thought away. What's done is done. Mink is dead, and he left me with an unexpected gift. An unexpected problem.

Going down the aisles, I pick out an enormous amount of socks and underwear, giving the funny little designs on the novelty socks a stony stare. I pick out five pairs of the warmest jeans and leggings I can find, raising an eyebrow at how thin the winter wear is for women. I stick a finger into one of the pockets and wonder how it's possible for them to even carry a phone.

By the time I'm finished with the clothes section, I have a large, warm green jacket, a thick yellow sweater, a handful of comfortable t-shirts, two pairs of boots—one with heels, one without—a pair of mittens and a pair of gloves, a wide-brimmed hat, large sunglasses, and a gray scarf that looks similar to mine. It's going to be a cold winter, and she'll need all she can get.

I check out at one of the self-checkout booths to avoid dealing with a cashier, and after feeding the machine cash, I head out and drive to a home improvement store.

Half an hour later, I'm loading tools and wood into my trunk.

As I do, something catches my attention from the corner of my eye.

There's a man leaning back against a black sedan two parking spaces down from me, smoking and pretending not to be watching me.

My jaw clenches. It wouldn't be suspicious to an ordinary person, but I'm savvy enough to know what his presence means.

There aren't many people in the parking lot this early, and I'm parked far out enough that nobody else is paying attention. In my head, I'm already planning out the different directions this could take.

The man makes brief eye contact with me. His cigarette isn't even lit, just hanging in his mouth.

I decide a direct approach is best.

"Need a light?" I grunt at him, my face stony.

He doesn't say anything. He gives the area a quick glance before he starts to approach me. I take a deep breath as I rest my hands on the top of my open trunk, and I put a hand down into one of my bags as the man gets near.

"Think you know we need to go for a ride, Sal-" he starts to say.

I cut him off with the ball peen hammer that I swing up, hitting his jaw with a sharp *crack* and sending him staggering.

Before he can fall, I catch him by the scruff of his collar and put his head down into the trunk of my car. I grab the trunk door and slam it down as hard as I can, and I hear another sickening crack of bone before he slumps to the ground and I shut the trunk in earnest.

It takes me all of two seconds to jump into the driver's seat, turn the ignition, and drive away, leaving him on the ground alone.

My plan is to just drive out calmly as not to attract attention.

The sedan the man had been leaning against peels out, and I realize his backup has other plans.

I gun the acceleration and take off toward the highway leading west out of town, not wanting to lead them anywhere near the safe house. The black sedan is on me in an instant.

I weave through neighborhoods, heading for the more run-down parts of town where it's less likely that the police will have patrolmen out to catch onto us. The last thing I need is the cops on me as well.

I've studied maps of Rochester, and it doesn't take me long to get out of the city.

And as I expected, as soon as we're out of a residential area, I hear the first gunshots.

My engine roars, and I weave in and out of the few other cars on the highway before I can turn off onto a wooded road. The sedan has a hard time keeping up with me, but once we're on a long stretch of wooded road, they don't need to—bullets start whizzing past the car, and I hear one hit the back.

I lower myself and get ready, and just as we come up to a bend in the road, I turn the wheel and grab the handbrake, turning the opposite direction of the bend.

The sedan slams on its brake, but they're still firing at me. A bullet pings off the metal on the front of the car as the sedan zooms past me, and they cut left so hard that the car flips over and rolls once into the ditch off the side of the road.

Immediately, I grab the gun from my glove box and get out of the car, aiming for the sedan, and two men spill out of it immediately.

One already has his gun out, and he gets a shot off before he even has his bearings.

It's a blind fire, but he gets lucky, and I feel a burning pain as it grazes my left arm. I don't show pain in the slightest, though, even as I feel warm blood start to wet my clothes.

With machine-like precision, I set my sights on

his head and fire once. A hole appears in his forehead, and he crumples to the ground.

The other man isn't fast enough to get his gun before I'm at the car, and he dives behind it, dodging my shot.

I don't give him a moment to recoup.

Hopping over the hood, I slide toward him, but he throws open the door to knock me off-balance.

I stagger, and he takes the chance to throw a punch at me. I lean back to avoid it, but the flash of light shows off his brass knuckles he has gripped in his hand, and the metal strikes me despite my dodging.

I feel blood run down my face.

When I come back in from the dodge, my own fist catches him in the stomach. He tries to get away, but I drop the gun and grab him by the brass-knuckled-wrist, squeezing it until it breaks as I use my other fist to start pummeling his ribs, feeling bones crack.

I don't feel anger, just instinct.

I bring my fist up across his jaw, then throw him against his own car, giving me enough time to pick up my gun and point it at him.

"Fucking traito-" he starts to say, but I silence him with a single shot through the eye.

He slumps against the car and to the ground, leaving me alone with the sound of my breath.

I put my gun away, then check their cell phones

to see if they've had time to message their bosses in the city. The last messages are from before I left the store.

I'm safe.

For now.

But soon enough, they'll be noticed to be missing, and their boss will know where I am. Not precisely, but way too close for comfort.

Nonetheless, I take the time to load the bodies into the trunk of their car, gloves on, and I get the car moved into the woods, behind enough brush that it will be some time before their bodies are found.

With that done, I get into my car as if nothing has happened.

Killing is an instinct for me, nothing more. I feel no resentment for those men. I may as well have just been caught in a traffic jam.

But as I pull off and start driving back toward the safe house, it takes a few minutes for me to remember the bullet wound I got on my arm. The warm blood is soaking through my clothes, and before I know it, I start to feel dizzy as I drive.

"Fuck," I mutter under my breath.

I need to get back. Fast.

EVA

I have been so conflicted all morning. When I woke up this morning to find myself in a comfortable bed in a house—albeit a house I hardly recognized—instead of on that rickety mattress in the bunker, a wave of relief washed over me.

That is, until I heard the scuffling of someone moving around in the living room. It all came rushing back to me. Sal coming into the bunker to save me. Leading me out into the sunshine. Making me food. Avoiding all my pointed questions. Going to bed wearing his clothes, which smelled just like him. Masculine and warm.

And my dream, the memory still lingering in the back of my mind, the phantom sensation of his kiss on my throat still so prominent in my mind. Even with the dark realization that he might be someone far worse than I could imagine.

But what else can I do? The last time I went to the police... It was terrible. I met a man at the restaurant, and we started flirting. He invited me back to his place, and I thought: *why not? I never let myself have any fun.*

Once we got there, though, he changed. His hands were on me, and it was only lucky that I was able to escape him. That time, I fled right to the police, and their barrage of questions.

How well did you know him? Sounds like it was just a date, are you sure you weren't giving off the wrong signals? He probably just misunderstood. Well, you did go back to his place after 10pm, what did you expect he wanted?

My stomach lurches at the memories, and I try to shake them away.

No, the cops wouldn't be able to help me. Especially if my kidnapper is nowhere to be found. Who would I even tell them took me? And the way Sal dodged my questions... he doesn't want to answer a lot of questions about where my kidnapper is.

I was always the girl that tried to play safe. To keep to herself, head down, always working. And look what that got me.

For once, I'm going to go for what I actually want. Trying to avoid danger has never saved me from it. So maybe taking a risk, and accepting fate's gift is what I need to heal.

Suddenly, I need to be near him. It's like a magnetic pull, dragging me out of bed and to his side. I walk into the living room and see him packing a bag, fully dressed and serious.

He glances at me, a smile coming to his lips as darkness swirls in his gaze. It's beautiful.

"Where are you going?"

"There are things you need if you're going to stay here."

"How do you know I'm going to stay?"

He looks at me, his eyes narrowing a little. "I already told you. It isn't safe for you to leave."

"But you never told me why. Why should I trust you?"

He sighs, looking at me, taking a step closer before something holds him back from closing the distance between us.

"Because. I will protect you. Things are... complicated."

"Complicated because you took care of the man that kidnapped me?"

"Yes."

"Sal... you saved me. I... I wouldn't get you in trouble. You're a hero."

His eyes rage with that storm once more, and he closes the distance, cupping my face in his hardened hand. I can feel every callous, every rough spot from his renovations, every little scar with such intensity, and it sends a shiver through me. I haven't been touched in so long, and it feels so good.

When I open my eyes again, he has a curious expression on his face, watching me.

It's almost as though he can read my thoughts, see that desire churning in my body, and I draw in my lower lip nervously. For a second, I think he's going to kiss me, and my heart races in anticipation. I let my lower lip go, glistening from my mouth, trying to tempt him to do just that.

But he resists the urge and heads towards the door.

"Just stay here. It's not safe for you out there yet, but I'll be back soon. And then we can figure out what to do."

"What to do... with me?"

He stares at me for a second, shaking his head.

"Just what to do, Eva. You're safe here. Protected. Let me keep protecting you."

He closes the door before I can reply, and I look around at my newfound freedom. I check each of the rooms, looking for any sign of my captor, but I don't find anything, and I find I'm exhausted, so I go to the kitchen and begin cooking. Nothing fancy, but it's not from a can, so it's practically heaven.

Every now and then, I catch myself thinking about running away. After all, I'm alone in the house.

It's not like Sal can keep me locked up here forever. It's not even like I want to be locked in here forever.

But I don't want to leave. I know nothing about Sal, but he's fascinating to me. He doesn't talk non-stop about sports or the latest new toy he bought. He's skilled with his hands...

A pleasant chill runs through me at that thought.

All my time in the bunker, I refused to touch myself, to find comfort in arousal and orgasm. I denied all my urges, no matter how much my fantasies took me into another world of pleasure and lust.

I know it seems sick to even be thinking about those things when I was locked in a bunker, but I was trapped with nothing to occupy my mind other than fears of the darkness I'd find once that door opened for me and my captor took me once more. Pleasant fantasies of a normal life was what kept me sane.

But now I find myself pent-up, and fantasizing about Sal's lips on my neck, then going lower, and lower.

I shake my head, forcing myself out of my reverie. I don't know anything about Sal.

For all I know, he could be an associate of the pervert who brought me here

But I don't feel that from him. I don't see him being that kind of man. Still, though, with his demeanor and hulking frame, there's no way Sal is just an accountant or a salesman or something. There's a streak of danger about him, something I should fear.

I know I should.

I have to be careful.

But I spent the night, and he never touched me. Just a dreamed kiss, and a pleasant sensation between my legs, and then the fear of who he really is. He was a perfect gentleman. Or at least one of the best I've met, as terrible as that is to say.

How odd it is to trust someone implicitly. As a rule, I never trust anyone fully. I keep everyone at arm's length, just in case they could hurt me. I've spent my whole life that way, afraid to let anyone get close to me. But Sal is different. He saved me. He took care of me. He's looking out for me when no one else will.

If I were smart, I would figure out a way to escape, to return to the real world and try and get my life back on track. Shouldn't I? Surely I can't just spend the rest of my life hiding out in this farm-house, hiding from facing the world and their horrible judgments.

But every time I think about leaving, I feel this twinge of fear. This longing for something. No, someone. I don't know if it is just my extreme lone-liness or disorientation at being suddenly freed after weeks underground, but I just can't bear the thought of leaving Sal. And I get the sense he doesn't want me to leave either, though I have no idea why.

"Get a grip," I tell myself aloud as I sit by the window, watching the gravel road overgrown with weeds. "You have no reason to feel loyal to him. He didn't come here looking for you. He just happened to come across you. Right place, right time. Nothing more."

But I can't get myself to agree with that. Maybe it is just fate. What do I have to go back to in Rochester? I've been gone for weeks with no warning. My bosses have long since given up on me. I've been fired, for sure. I have no real friends, my mom's been gone for years, and I never did get myself that cat I wanted. Nobody depends on me. Nobody misses me. Unless you count my father, who has supposedly suddenly decided he wants me in his life out of nowhere.

I don't count him.

I'm sure my disappearance has gone unnoticed. I might as well be nobody. But for as long as I can manage it, at least I can be a nobody with Sal. No one else has ever shown me the kind of patience and gentleness he showed me yesterday, not since my mother died and left me alone in the world.

The man who saved me from the sickest fates imaginable. It's like a fairytale, isn't it?

I halfheartedly chuckle, thinking of my life winding up like a fairytale. From rags to riches, isn't that the dream? And Sal doesn't seem rich. He just seems... right.

Which is why it's been so difficult waiting for him to come back. What if he's abandoning me? What if 'going to town for supplies' was just his ruse to get out of dodge?

"No," I tell myself. "He wouldn't do that to me. He promised he wouldn't leave."

And just as I'm saying that, I hear the faint rumble of tires on gravel. I jump up, my heart pounding away as I stare out the window. Sal's sleek, shiny black car comes rolling up to the house and I bolt away to the front door, pushing it open and running outside. I can't wait to be close to him again. I need him. Desperately.

The car rolls to a stop and I stand there in my oversized T-shirt and boxers, barefoot, my hair a wild mess and my heart thumping, waiting for my savior to get out and return to me. When the door pushes open, Sal slowly gets out, standing tall even as he clutches a strip of blood-soaked fabric to his left bicep. My stomach turns and I gasp, clapping a hand over my mouth. Then I see his face. There's a bloody scratch under his right eye, a purplish bruise blooming on his cheek. He's hurt. And it does not look good.

"Oh my god!" I cry out, rushing over to him. "Were you in an accident?" I look at the vehicle, noting not a scratch on the front, nothing that seems off really. He's stoic and unruffled as always, looking down at me with those solemn, dark brown eyes. There's pain there, and a twinge of regret. "What happened?" I demand to know, reaching up to gingerly touch his cheek. He doesn't shy away from my touch, but he reaches up to take my hand and give it a squeeze.

"It doesn't matter. I will be fine," he assures me in that low growl. "There are bags in the back seat. Can you grab them?"

I shake my head fiercely. "Yes, I can. But no, you can't just brush this off, Sal. You're injured. Come inside and let me look at your wounds, okay? I can help you."

"You can?" he asks dubiously, one dark eyebrow raised.

I grab the bags from the backseat, then take his hand and start pulling him toward the front door.

"Yes. I can. I've been taking night classes to become a nurse. Or at least I was. I guess they've probably kicked me out of the course by now, I've missed so many assignments," I sigh, fully realizing this loss for the first time. "But don't worry. I was the top of my class while I was still enrolled. I know what to do."

At least, I hope I do, I think to myself. I hurry Sal inside, leading him into the kitchen, as it's the cleanest, most sanitary room of the house. I instruct him to sit down at the table. I kneel down beside him, peeling away the bloody fabric he's been pressing against his arm to staunch the blood flow. He holds it there, almost like he doesn't want me to see the injury.

I look up at his face with my lips pursed.

"Your color is still good, and you seem fully cognizant, so it doesn't look like you've lost too much blood," I remark. "But you have to let me look at the wound. I need to make sure it's not going to get infected."

Reluctantly, he pulls the strip away and I try not to gasp at the bloody gash on his arm. It doesn't look like a wound from a car accident. It looks more like a gunshot wound, but it's not deep enough. Besides, how the hell would he have gotten into a gunfight? He was hardly gone for several hours!

"Sal," I breathe, clucking my tongue sympathetically. "That looks awfully painful."

He shrugs, an unadvisable move for someone with an injured arm. "It's not bad. I have certainly had worse than that."

I look up at him, furrowing my brows in confusion. "You've had worse than... this?"

He clams up, clearly under the impression that he's said too much already. Getting information out of this guy is like pulling teeth.

"You know, you may be the one person on the planet more emotionally closed-off than I am," I comment, getting up to grab a damp paper towel. I wet it in the sink and come back to dab lightly at the wound. I brace myself for him to jerk away at the pain, but he doesn't even flinch. It's like he doesn't feel pain. He doesn't feel anything at all, it appears.

"Doesn't that hurt?" I inquire, carefully wiping away dried blood. I get up and grab the whole roll of paper towels, getting to work. Sal sits stiffly, watching me out of the corner of his eye. I can tell that he's not accustomed to anyone fussing over him like this.

"It doesn't hurt much," he admits finally. "Just a twinge."

"So, are you going to tell me how the hell this happened? Or do I have to guess?" I ask.

Sal sighs. "It's nothing for you to worry about."

"Look, you saved my life, and now I'm going to patch you up. I think we owe each other a little more information. A little more… vulnerability," I suggest, blushing. I can't think of a better word for what I want from him. He scoffs.

"You really want to know?" he says flatly.

I nod. "Yes. It will help me determine how best to treat the wound."

"It was a bullet."

"What?" I burst out, dropping my paper towel to the floor. I reach for another one, this time to dab at the cut under his eye. He tries to move away from me but I catch him.

"It barely grazed my arm. No big deal," he says, shrugging.

"No big…" I trail off, shaking my head. "Sal. Someone shot you."

"They missed."

"Not entirely!" I exclaim, pointing at his arm.

"Just a scrape," he remarks. I roll my eyes.

"Okay. So a bullet just lightly scraped your arm. What about your face? What happened here? Don't tell me it was another bullet that just happened to scrape your face," I say, folding my arms over my chest. He looks reluctant to answer, but I just stare at him until he gives in.

"This was a fist."

"A… sharp fist?" I press him, gesturing to the scratch.

"A fist wearing a sharp ring," he adds.

"Okay, now we're getting somewhere," I say. "Whose fist was it? Who did this to you?"

Sal closes his mouth and gives me a defiant look. I stand up, scooping the paper towels into my hands to dump them in the trash and start over with fresh ones. I pull up a chair and sit in front of Sal, imploring him with my eyes.

"You're really not going to tell me," I mutter in frustration.

"Why do you want to know so badly?" he asks softly.

"Because I just do!" I exclaim, throwing up my

hands. "Look, it's been a weird month, okay? You know that. I was trapped in some creepy pervert's lair for weeks. Then you found me. You saved me, Sal. And you're not a cop. You're not a detective. You're a stranger who just happened to find me, and now we're both hiding here in this dilapidated house like squatters and you won't tell me anything about yourself."

"We're not squatting," he says.

"What?" I ask, rubbing the bridge of my nose.

"We aren't squatters here. I own the property. I bought it under foreclosure."

"Really? Out of everything I just said, *that's* the part you're going to answer?" I complain. He gives me a faint smile.

"You're asking a lot of questions, but I don't know anything about you, either," he says.

"Fine. What do you want to know? I'm an open book," I tell him, leaning back in the chair. Sal fixes me with a dubious expression. "What? I'm serious. Go ahead. Ask away."

"Where are you from?" he asks.

"Rochester."

"Do you know the name of the man who brought you here? How do you know him? Or rather, how does he know you?" he asks.

I bite my lip.

"I don't know his name. And I had never met him before. I think he just chose me at random. He saw the opportunity to take me, and he did. It was just a case of being at the wrong place at the wrong time. I've had bad luck all my life, this is no different."

Sal doesn't look satisfied with that answer, but he moves on. "Why do you say you have bad luck?"

I groan, rolling my eyes. "Okay, this isn't fair. I'm asking simple, pertinent questions and you're demanding my life story."

"Bad luck is your life story?" he says pointedly.

I blush, feeling both exposed and frustrated. I know why I'm asking all these questions. I'm starved for conversation, for closeness. Hell, I've been locked away with no contact with the outside world for nearly a month. Of course I'm a little needy. It doesn't mean anything. Does it?

"I have another question," I say softly. "And it's an important one."

Sal looks concerned, his upper lip twitching, "Ask it."

"Why do you want me to stay here? What's going on? Why can't I leave?" I ask, looking up at him through my lashes. I'm afraid of the answer. I'm afraid of his reaction. But he just looks at me, sizing me up.

"That's not something I can answer just yet," he says slowly.

"Why the hell not? You know, I trust you, Sal. God damn it, I know I shouldn't. But I do. You say it's not safe for me to leave, and even though I should be suspicious of you, I'm not. I believe you. But you can't even give me a straight answer as to why?" I demand.

"It would put you in danger. It's just not safe for you, or us. There will be time for that... later on," he says.

"Ugh!" I groan, cradling my face in my hands. Then I look back up at him, frustrated tears burning in my eyes. "Sal, who are you?"

His eyes are sorrowful. Apologetic. Like he wants to say more, but he can't. I lean in closer, dabbing at the spot under his eye. Both his wounds are closing up nicely, neatly. Even the bruise on his cheek seems to be going down. There's that same intense heat radiating off of him, the air between us somehow imbued with electricity. I'm so annoyed with him, and yet all I can think about is how I want to get closer. Press myself against him. Share that warmth and bask in his glow. I want him to make me feel alive again.

His dark eyes glance down at my lips, just for a moment. Barely noticeable, but just enough to make my heart skip a beat.

But he remains silent.

There's scarcely two inches between us. I swear I can hear his heart beating, slow and steady compared to my hummingbird rhythm.

"You won't let me leave, and you won't give me

any answers, either," I murmur, shaking my head. "Sal, what can you give me?"

He reaches to cup my face gently with his huge hand and I lean into his touch. Then, without thinking twice about it, I lean forward and press my lips against his, sending a shock of electric pleasure down my spine.

*E*verything inside me is screaming that I need to bring this to a screeching halt. My mind is telling me that this is wrong, that I shouldn't be going this far with this broken girl, that I'm going into ruin her forever by crossing this threshold with her.

But our bodies want it. God, do they want it.

I feel her shiver run up her body from her warm, soft lips. I'd be lying if I said I haven't thought about her, about how she feels and tastes. But I've always kept those feelings in tight check. I don't need to further complicate this already tricky situation.

Those thoughts are melting away as she sighs into me.

She's wanted this. She's probably thought about it more than I have.

I could stop her. I could push her away and send

her to her bed alone, leave the house for a few hours, find a quiet place in the woods to relieve the tension she's built up in my pants.

But I don't.

Her hands go to my shoulders and squeeze the hard, bulging muscles that run from my neck to my biceps. Her fingers trace ever so delicately along the wound she's just treated. It stings sweetly to her touch, and I don't stop her.

When she realizes I'm not thrusting her away, she slides the chair away from under her as she comes forward and puts her legs around me, sitting in my lap.

She still hasn't broken the damn kiss.

Her tongue playfully tests my lips, begging to come in deeper. I don't let her at first. I move my lips to her cheek and feel her soft skin, and she gasps as she starts to gently grind against me.

There's no finesse to what she's doing. She's all pure, animalistic desire. Her fingers are greedy, and they hold onto my shoulders. She brings her lips back to mine and pleads for me.

I kiss her more aggressively. This time, she's not the one making the first move, it's me. My tongue intrudes into her lips, grazing her teeth and meeting her tongue for just a moment before I come back, and she follows me.

While we play these games with our mouths, she touches my face with both hands, holding my jaw in her palms and caressing it. My skin is clean shaven, but she manages to find every bump of stubble she can. Her thumbs brush against the edges of my jaw, and her fingers curl in.

She slides a hand behind my head and grips a handful of my thick, coarse hair. She seems to savor every inch of it she can feel. I hear her breathing in, and I know she's taking in the subtle scent of my cologne.

She's so desperate for human touch, to know what another person feels like, tastes like, smells like. A week in isolation feels like a year. A month must feel like a lifetime.

It's been so long since I've had a woman in my lap that I've forgotten what it feels like. I'm suddenly weak to Eva's charms, to the softness of her body, to the passion in her motions. I've been feared as the *Angel of Death* for a decade, maybe longer. All I met knew my reputation. But she doesn't know me at all. I know that, because she doesn't fear me.

And for once in my life, I'm grateful that someone isn't afraid of me.

Her hips are shameless in how they grind against my lap. I feel her warm and needy through the thin fabric of my own boxers.

The thought of her getting wet inside my clothes and grinding up against them makes my cock grow thicker.

I've been able to have any woman I've wanted

over the years. Maybe it's something about my height or my commanding gaze, but I've been able to bend anyone I want to my will, gladly, even though they fear me in the same breath that they say they want me.

If that's true of most people, it's desperately true of Eva.

I never wanted any of them. Not until I met her. Darkness clouds my vision, lust propelling me on, even past the point that I know I should stop her. A damaged girl, someone sweet who needs protection.

But she doesn't have a protector. All she has is me.

She hasn't stopped moving, squirming on me. She presses her chest to mine. Her nipples are already stiff inside my shirt. I feel her heart beating at a mile a minute.

Finally, our kiss breaks long enough for her to take a few desperate breaths, and she looks into my eyes with a gaze that melts even my icy heart. It's full of desire and need, but there's a plea in it, too.

"Salvatore," she pronounces my full name, slowly, letting each syllable linger on those lips that have gotten puffy and red since we've spent time attacking each other. "Do you know how badly I need this?"

"You're not thinking straight," I say in a deep, husky voice, moving to stand. She wraps her arms around my neck and thrusts her hips against me desperately, not letting me go.

"Please, Sal," she urges me, the whimper in her words so thick I could cut it with a knife.

"How long has it been?" I ask, my black eyes holding her paralyzed. She's utterly wrapped around my finger, and I've only known her a short time.

She hesitates, and she worries her lip, a sudden look of fear in her eyes.

"... Never," she admits at last as her hands slide to my sides. But when she feels how hard and rippling my torso is, she lets them explore further, going around to my back so that she can pull herself into me more. Her inner thighs are against my hips, and every time she slides into me, I can feel that shiver of need roll through her.

My expression doesn't change, and I can tell that's making her squirm more.

I won't admit to her that the fact that she's never been with another man makes my heart beat harder, desire her even more.

It complicates everything.

Some part of me knows this is a terrible idea. I need to get her out of my life, out of my system. Yet I'm drawn to her. I want her, more than I've ever wanted anyone, or anything. I barely know her, but she's the most beautiful woman I've ever met, and that's hard to ignore.

Especially with the blood flowing in the wrong direction, away from my head.

Maybe this is what you need to keep her close to you. Away from the cops, the devil on my shoulder whispers in my ear, and I've never ignored that clever, cunning voice before. Especially not when I have Eva in my lap, all but pleading for my cock.

Slowly, I bring a hand up her hip, then slide it under the shirt she's wearing, and I feel the bare, hot skin underneath. I watch her, looking for any signs of discomfort, but she looks at me with such passion and desire, it's hard to resist.

My fingertips brush the underside of her breast, and her mouth starts to hang open before I even get to her nipple. When I touch it, it's already stiff, and it hardens for me.

"For a virgin," I say, letting the word linger on the tip of my tongue before letting it spill, watching her blush, "this is... surprising."

"When I was down there," she says through a strained gasp as I flick her nipple idly, starting to enjoy making her squirm at my slightest movement, "I... I never did anything."

"What was that?" I ask, covering her whole breast with my hand, and she draws in a sharp breath as if touched by fire.

"I..." she tries, struggling, "I never... to myself." She's still holding the words back, and it makes me smile. I've hardly noticed that my cock is rock-hard inside my pants, and her sensitive inner thigh is grinding against the bulging outline of it in my jeans.

"Say it," I command her, my voice smooth and dark.

She swallows, her gaze desperate. "I never touched myself while I was down there."

Of course she didn't. The gaze of an evil man was on her the whole time, she must have had some clue about that. And she definitely wasn't going to be in the mood.

But to already be a virgin, to have never known the most personal touch of another human being and then to go so long without a shred of release...

No wonder she's so helpless on my lap.

"Tell me more," I say. Now, I'm being cruel in how much I'm holding myself back. My hand is frozen over her breast, not giving her any of the stimulation she wants so badly. "Tell me what you wanted to do."

The virgin's blushing face alone could send me spilling over the edge, if I wanted to. The sight of that angelic face had sent my heart beating when I first saw it, but now, it has me almost dizzy with desire.

She opens her mouth to speak, but I silence it with a harsh kiss that earns a squeak of surprise before I move my mouth down to her neck to start teasing her sensitive skin with my teeth. "Say it."

"I wanted to touch myself," she moans softly,

barely more than a whisper. "I wanted to... to put my fingers between my lips and rub myself until I was wet. I thought about men so many nights…"

"Men?"

"Huge, strong men in my dreams," she confesses, "doing terrible things to me. I wanted it. I wanted it so badly, but I didn't want to give in."

Her words are surprisingly dark, and they make my blood rush. Maybe she can handle the darkness in my heart, if that's where her fantasies went under the most horrific circumstances. Perhaps she could come to truly be mine. If I claim her.

"You have some willpower," I say, amused. "What about now?"

"I want you, Salvatore," she whimpers, her voice nearly cracking from being so hungry for me. "I want to give in. I want this." As she lets the words out of her mouth, she pushes herself down against my cock as much as she can, and I feel it pulse and throb under her. It wants to feel her as badly as she wants it inside her.

"You don't know anything about me," I say, and my words carry as much weight as they need to. I reach behind her and take a fistful of her hair, holding it like a leash to tilt her head back and look up at me as I loom over her. "You're a good girl, aren't you, Eva?"

"If you want me to be," she whispers, and I smile at her efforts. I reward her my sliding my other hand to her ass and squeezing it, holding her hair a little tighter.

"I'm not a good man," I say.

"I don't care," she gasps. "I want you to ruin me."

I don't need any more invitation. Hand under her ass, I stand up, holding her firm against my waist.

If she wants to be mine, I will take her. It won't be the worst thing I've done this week. Hell, not even the worst thing I've done today.

I walk her over to the kitchen table and set her down on it. I grip the hem of her shirt and pull it off her before she can even gain her balance. She's topless in front of me, shocked at first, but she holds back her instincts to cover herself up. She looks up at me with a nervous gaze, as if hoping I'll find her pleasing.

I respond by putting my hands around her hips and my lips to her nipple, pushing her down onto her back and devouring her breast.

She lets out a moan of pleasure as I let my tongue lash out at her, tasting her stiff bud and moving to the other to do the same. My hands feel the soft flesh and squeeze, groping my way around her and taking in every inch of her body as mine.

I bought this house. Everything in it is mine. Including Eva.

When I've had my fill of tasting her breasts, I grip the boxers, and she helps me get them off her and toss them to the floor. The next moment, she's sprawled out before me, completely naked, me still with my clothes on, looming over her.

She looks up at me with a cherry-red blush, limbs squirming, watching me full of desire. She needs me. The mere sight of me is fulfilling every fantasy that's kept her warm in bed at night, made her wish for something, anything to fill her up.

I unbutton my pants, and I let out my cock.

It's long and hard, and the look Eva gives it tells me she's surprised by the girth of it. I stroke the shaft up and down with my large, heavy hand, and I let out a groan at the excitement even that simple touch brings me.

It has been a long time for me, too. Running from the law and the mafia, taking so many lives, gutting this house and building it to my own desires, it all let time get away from me.

Now, all I have is time. Time, and Eva.

"You've never had a man make you come?" I ask, my voice dark and gravelly through my thick lust as I feel her inner thighs with my rough hands. She shakes her head softly, looking up at me full of anticipation.

I smile.

"I'm going to take my time with you."

I hold her ankles up and place them over my shoulders, and I watch the anticipation well up into pure lust as I slide my cock along the wet, hot slit of her womanhood.

"I never knew it would be like this," she moans into the still air of the kitchen that's silent except for the sounds of our breathing.

"I'm not even in you yet," I growl, grinding the soft underside of my cock against her slit, back and forth, wetting both of us with the glistening honey coming from her. My cock gets stiffer at the touch of her.

She's softer than I could have imagined, more ready, more hot and wet than even my darkest desires could have wanted. And I've wanted her, I can't deny that.

She's already arched up onto me, but I hold her ass in my hands to push her up into me, putting her totally under my control, and I glower down at her, my eyes black as midnight.

"If you want me to stop," I say, "the safe word is 'ice.'"

She nods, understanding me, and I perch my huge crown on the edge of her swollen, puffy lips.

She has a view of me that includes the thick trunk of my shaft, the V that points down to it at my hips, the abs that ripple up my body, my broad pecs, and my face.

"This is your first time. I will be careful," I say, "but I can only be so gentle."

Without another word, I thrust my cock into her, and she lets out a sharp cry, tossing her head back and shuddering all around me.

"Fuck, you're tight," I say, and it's no lie. She's so tight I don't know whether I can fit my whole girth into her. Barely a third of me is inside her, and already, I feel her hot insides tightening around me.

I guide her hips as I start to rock back and forth, groaning into each one as I grip her ass, feeling her skin and its gentle give. She's so soft and naive, and I know she has no idea what she's truly getting into with me.

"Is it... is it too big?" she says between desperate gasps, eyes fluttering open and watching me go into her. Something about the sight of that from the table awakens something in her, though, and I feel my cock wetter than ever in her.

"We'll find out," I say, and as if at my command, her wetness lets me dive further into her. I'm where no one else has been before inside this girl. She feels tight and sweet, and I feel warmth traveling up my shaft and into my abdomen with every thrust.

"I thought about this," she confesses, hands gripping the table as she desperately tries to push herself up into me. "Oh my god, Sal, I thought about this the first time you found me."

Do you think I didn't?

I rock harder into her, getting bolder with each thrust that makes her get tighter and tighter, holding my cock closer the more I go into her, getting to her g-spot.

"I... I almost wanted you to take me in there!" she

breathes, absolutely drunk on lust for me, for my attention, my touch, my trust.

I push my hips in and up, and the tip of my cock grinds against her g-spot. The writhing and the gasp that she gives tell me that white-hot pleasure is searing through her, and I see tears welling up in those beautiful blue eyes and running down flawless cheeks.

I truly am making love to an angel, and I'm blissfully ruining her.

I start bucking into her and hitting that sweet spot over and over again, my veins bulging with the hot blood that's coursing through my shaft, all for her. She may be an angel, but the sin she draws out from me is all the sweeter.

Precum spills out of my shaft as I pulse and thrust into her over and over, pounding relentlessly into this treasure that I found buried underground. My body needs her. Even as my heavy balls strike her ass with each new thrust, getting tighter and more sore with need each time, everything about her feels right.

She's too good for this world, and what I'm doing is utter sin.

It takes no time at all for her eyes to clench tight and her pussy to tighten even more, wrapped firmly around my cock like they were meant for each other while I rub her g-spot over and over. I know that feeling well.

"Sal, I'm going to come!" she cries, her voice a needy whimper.

Her whole body gets tight, she reaches up to grip my wrists and dig her fingernails into my forearms, and when she comes, she lets out a long cry of ecstasy, dragging her nails down to my wrists as I feel her whole body go limp around me. She's melting into a hot mess, and I drove her there.

Her face is flushed, and so is her chest down to the top of her breasts.

When I pull my cock out of her, she's still breathing heavily, but she looks up with fear in her eyes as I do.

"Already? Did I do something wrong?"

"No," I say simply with a laughing smile. I give her no more explanation.

I get down on a knee, one hand massaging my cock, and I use the other to pull her close to me before I let my tongue out on her lower lips.

She draws in a hissing breath as I lick the honey from her, stroke after stroke, and she sticks her hands into my hair to hold onto me as I find her clit.

She tastes delicious, and I'm not wasting a drop of her.

Once I've cleaned her up and eased her down from her orgasm, I let my tongue flick out and hit her clit, and she arches her back all over again.

My tongue darts in and out, feeling that swollen, needy bud that's already so worked-up from her first orgasm that her body just lets everything flow, and all the wetness that I licked from her comes back to my face. It gets all over her sensitive inner thighs and my cheeks, and it's blissful.

Her taste is better than anything I could have imagined.

I let my tongue linger on her swollen clit, rolling back and forth on it, feeling its heat, every little twitch of desire that she shows with a thrust of her hips into me.

But an orgasm from the clit is different from an orgasm deeper within her, and soon, I can feel a new kind of pleasure building up inside the tightly-wound coil that is her body.

There's so much tension in her I keep finding, and my tongue is undoing all of it.

I'm relentless as I taste her, tormenting her nub with my tongue over and over again, lashing it, licking it, drawing out more of her honey until her fingers start to grip my head tighter.

Her hips buck up into me, and I feel her orgasm all around me with a sigh. I can't hold back a smile into her pussy as I keep licking her, not losing any momentum. She's all mine, and I'm going to show her that, thoroughly.

She tries to writhe and squirm in my grip, but my single hand has her in its control. My other hand strokes my shaft, the mere taste of her keeping me so stiff and ready for more action.

I feel another orgasm crash through her, and I soon lose count of how many little crests of pleasure I'm driving her through as I lick her. Sometimes I dive deep into her before coming back to the surface, but I spend most of it just on the cusp, teasing her and torturing her clit, and that alone is enough to push her over the edge.

By the time I can hear her panting, I decide it's time to give her a short break. I look up from her pussy over her breasts and smile at her, my face gleaming with *her.*

She looks down at me, so defeated, but I stand up and she sees the length of my cock still stiff and taut.

"You're... you're still...?" she pants in disbelief.

"For you," I growl.

I pull her to the edge of the table and sit her up. Her body is nearly helpless in my hands. I can do whatever I want with her.

I lean in and kiss her deeply, letting her taste all of my lips and my tongue.

"Do you taste that?" I whisper in a dark tone, and she nods softly. "That's you on me. Your taste. Your scent." I lean in to her ear and breathe, "Proof that you're *mine.*"

She nods again, a breathy gasp this time, and I scoop her up in my arms to go back to the chair where this hot mess all began.

I turn her around so that her back is facing me,

and I slowly let her slide down onto my cock as I sit down.

It had been different when I was on top of her—now, there's nothing to protect her from gravity doing its work and spearing her on me.

My cock immediately rubs up against her g-spot, every inch of my girth stuffed into her so tight I wonder if it's hurting her, but she wiggles her hips, feeling as much of me as she can.

"Sal," she sighs, the word a blissful note on her voice, "Sal, this is incredible, I-"

I reach around her and cup her breasts in my hands, silencing her as my fingers toy with her nipples and my breath rolls onto her neck.

"You are incredible," I breathe thickly. "You feel incredible."

I thrust my hips up into her, my cock pulsing, and she lets her head fall back onto my shoulder. I'm her rock and her captor all at once. She pushes her ass up against me, and that just makes my cock get stiffer inside her. My bulging head rubs up against her already ravaged g-spot. Her body twists and writhes on my cock, but now that I have her like this, nothing can save her from me.

Within minutes, she starts to get tight again, and I kiss away the tears of bliss that are rolling down her cheeks as I start to buck up harder and harder into her.

Soon, I'm practically bouncing this sweet, innocent, broken woman on my cock. It's wrong to take her, but nothing within me can resist it. I want to come inside her, feel our fluids together, absolutely let go of all my inhibitions with her.

She doesn't know what to do with her legs. She tries wrapping them around mine, or the chair legs, but in the end, she lets them go limp and helpless as I fuck up into her. She can feel every muscle on me, from my pecs to my rock-hard thighs, and she leans into it all, letting herself get pinned against my cock.

Finally, her ecstasy takes her by surprise, and she yelps as I feel wetness on my cock yet again, fresh honey dousing me. She reaches back and holds onto the chair, actually trying to push herself down further onto me as I feel her get tighter and hotter before relaxing and unwinding on me, every muscle in her body twitching with utter pleasure, tension melting away like butter. She slumps back onto the wall that is my chest and lets her grip go, leaving me alone to hold her up and feel her.

I open my mouth to tell her my plans for her, but to my surprise, even though she's panting and breathless, she manages to beat me to the punch. She turns her head, lidded eyes looking at me hungrily.

"I want to taste your cock," her innocent voice says, dripping with the sinful lust that I've plunged her into.

EVA

"Can I? Please?" I ask timidly, standing up and turning to face Sal. He's looking at me with those solemn, dark eyes, searching my face.

Every time he looks at me this way, it gives me a little shiver. I feel so exposed, so vulnerable, and not just because I'm naked. His gaze seems to tear away at the walls built up around me, stripping down all my excuses and reasons for keeping my heart hidden away under lock and key. He burns down the tall hedges around my soul, staring down into the deepest, darkest, most secret corners of who I am. Like he can somehow understand me, see my thoughts before I even think them.

It's both terrifying and thrilling at the same time. I have never met anyone who seems to understand me, predict me. I don't know how he does it, but it almost feels like I don't even need words. I just need his touch. He tells me all of this when he looks at me.

All in one intense gaze.

He reaches for my hands and I bite my lip, looking down at his massive cock, still glistening with my honey. My pussy aches to have him inside me again, filling me up, stuffing me full until I'm bursting. But I want to try something different. Something I have never done before. I'm not totally naive; I've seen dirty movies, read a dirty novel or two in my day. I know how it's supposed to work. But I'm new at this, and I want to experience it all.

Sal pulls me forward to kiss my lips, cupping my face in his huge hands.

That's what surprises me most about him. The strange little acts of tenderness that contrast so much with his hard stare, his gruff words. Maybe that's what I see in him, a gentleness lying dormant beneath the surface of his hardened heart.

I sense that he's broken too.

Maybe our broken pieces can fit together.

He gently nudges me down. I dutifully kneel on the tile floor between his thighs as he sits on the chair, looking at me. I glance up at him, my heart fluttering nervously.

"I just want to make you feel good," I tell him, blushing. He nods.

"Go ahead," he urges me, stroking the hair back out of my face and tucking it behind my ears. He traces my bottom lip with his thumb and pushes it inside for a moment, a tantalizing preview of what's to come when there is something much bigger in my mouth. Just having his thumb between my lips sends a spiral of pleasure down my body and suddenly I need the real thing. I can't wait any longer.

I lean forward and part my lips, gently kissing the swollen head of his shaft, looking up at Sal all the while to gauge his reaction. He's patient. Waiting for more. I wrap both hands around the enormous length of his cock and begin to slide them up and down slowly while I pull more of him into my mouth. It's so big I can feel my mouth stretching to accommodate him, the sensation of my cheeks aching and my tongue swirling around the sensitive head making me wet.

I moan as I push down, taking more and more into my mouth as I reach down to caress his sack. Sal lets out a low groan, leaning his head back. His hands come down to tangle in my hair, guiding me, pushing me further down until I'm nearly choking myself on his massive cock, the head just lightly brushing the ticklish back of my throat.

I begin to move faster, sucking his cock enthusiastically. It feels incredible, bobbing up and down on Sal's massive, glorious shaft while he gently rolls his hips up to meet my rhythm, like he just can't help it. Like I'm making him feel so fucking good he can't even be still.

"Just like that, Eva," he growls, pushing down on the back of my head, guiding me. I moan around his impressive length, my tongue flicking along the sensitive underside of his cock. "So fucking good, sweetheart," he says softly.

I glance up to see his eyes closed and his jaw tightening. He's trying his very best to restrain himself. I can tell he wants so badly to lose control and fuck my mouth with abandon. And I want him to do that. I want him to use me, thrust into my throat until I'm gagging.

Still pumping his cock with both hands, I release him with a wet pop and look up at him, licking my lips.

"I want you to use me," I tell him. His eyes open and he gazes down at me, a little taken aback by my words. I can't help but blush, but I don't back down even for a second.

"You want…" he trails off. I nod.

"Fuck my throat," I murmur. "Please. I want you to feel good."

"Are you sure you can handle it?" he asks, sounding genuinely concerned. His worry for me is sweet and appreciated, but it's not what I need right now. In this moment, I don't want Sal soft and cautious. I want him ravenous and forceful. I want him to relinquish the control he's been tightly clinging to.

"Don't be afraid to hurt me. I can handle it," I tell

him earnestly. "Don't hold back. You can… you can come in my mouth if you want," I add, my cheeks burning. I'm not used to talking to anyone this way. I don't think I have ever even *thought* words like this before, much less said them aloud to another person.

I never knew this side of me existed. Desperate. Needy. Turned on beyond belief, begging for pleasure in the shape of punishment. It almost scares me, that Sal could elicit such a response from me.

Who the hell am I anymore?

How did that bunker change me?

I decide that's a question for future me. Right now, I just don't fucking care.

Sal's teeth are gritted together, those solemn eyes watching me as though he's expecting to take it all back, to change my mind and back away from him in fear. But I've said my piece. I've asked for exactly what I want. I bend down to pull his cock back into my mouth, sucking him harder, bobbing up and down as I look up at him with pleading eyes. I want him to understand how serious I am, how badly I need this. More than even he needs it, I'm certain.

"Once I begin, I can't guarantee I'll be able to stop," he says finally, his voice low and serious. Warning me that I'm about to step over the edge of a cliff. There's no going back. "I'm going to fuck your mouth, and then I'm going to fuck your tight little pussy again until you scream. It might hurt. I won't hold back."

I nod, begging him with my eyes. This is what I want.

After a moment of silent deliberation, Sal stands up, reaching down to cup the back of my head with one hand while he holds onto the table to steady himself with the other. His fingers wrap into my hair and I'm salivating, desperate for him to use me the way he promised to.

And then, he does.

He pushes my face down on his cock, pressing into my throat while I moan. He thrusts into me harder and faster, slamming into my mouth. I'm so fucking wet I can feel my juices dripping down my bare thighs as I choke on Sal's massive cock, reveling in the sensation of my cheeks aching and my throat ticklish, threatening to gag me.

Gripping a fistful of my hair, he snaps his hips back and forth, his long, hard shaft sliding in and out of my mouth. The only thing I can do is struggle to keep my mouth wide open and hold on for dear life, wrapping my arms around his legs as he fucks my throat harder and harder. It's glorious, exhilarating, feeling his slick rod ramming into my throat. I can't stop moaning, my legs shaking and my cunt pulsing, desperate to be touched.

"Oh, you're so good," Sal groans. "I love your fucking mouth. Stretch those pretty lips for me, Eva."

He's like a well-oiled machine, all hard angles and

powerful muscle underneath that smooth, olive skin. I can feel him starting to lose control, his rhythm getting more and more erratic, as though he's getting ready to blow. I can't decide what I'd like better: tasting his come as it slides down my throat, or feeling him pump my pussy full of his seed so it can slowly leak out of me after.

Either way, I need him to come. I need to make him explode.

I can taste a few drops of his come in my mouth, sweet and bitter at the same time. I'm not totally innocent. I know this can happen before a man orgasms. And it's like a little taster, a teaser of what's in store. I need more, to pump every last drop from his incredible cock.

It's like he can read my mind, because suddenly, he pulls away and yanks me up to my feet. Then he picks me up with such ease I might as well be a feather, and lays me back onto the table. Sal grabs my legs and hooks them up over his shoulders, positioning the engorged head of his shaft at my glistening pussy. With no preamble, he slides inside me, all the way down to the hilt, making me cry out with pleasure.

"Oh my god. Oh my god," I mumble, my arms flailing out on either side of me to grasp the edges of the table and keep myself steady as Sal slams into my aching, needy cunt. Every thrust sends a shock wave of bliss through my body, and at this angle, he can strike my g-spot every single time. Even on the rare occasion that I have touched myself, I never managed to find that spot. Sometimes I used to think I might be defective, that maybe it was missing.

But it turns out, I just needed the right person to find it. And Sal has certainly found it. Again and again and again.

My mind, for the first time in almost a month, goes silent. All my fears, all my dread that had been wound up around my heart simply fades away. I thought I would die a virgin, alone, afraid. But Sal has given me new life. Even as he makes my body ache, fucking me hard, I thrill at the sensations. Because they're mine. They're something other than horror, something other than pitiful tears.

Passion sparks between us, each seeking something in the other's body.

He pounds into me with his stiff cock, my thighs trembling as he reaches up to caress my breasts, rolling my sensitive, perky nipples between his fingers. With every touch, I get closer and closer to climax, until finally my pussy clenches up around his shaft and I explode into orgasm.

"Oh, fuck! Sal!" I scream, gushing sweet honey all over his cock. He doesn't let up for even a second, fucking me harder and harder while I squirm beneath him.

"That's what I like to hear," he growls, reaching

down to circle my overly-sensitive clit while he fucks my g-spot over and over again. The combined sensation is too much, too overwhelming, and I almost recoil from it. I've never felt this fucking good before. I didn't even know it was possible for sex to feel like this. Even in my wildest fantasies, I never imagined anything quite like this.

"Oh god," I pant, closing my eyes and losing myself to the pounding rhythm of his thrusts deep inside me. My pussy is so wet, I can feel my juices sliding down my ass, making a little puddle on the table. Sal shows no mercy, his stiff cock slamming into me so quickly, I can't even keep up with it. I'm like a ragdoll, limp and lost in a sea of pleasure as he thrusts deep within me.

"Fuck, you're so goddamn tight," he murmurs through gritted teeth. Then, he adds imperiously, "Tell me how it feels, Eva. I want to know what my cock is doing to you."

I struggle to breathe and think clearly, my brain is so overcome with pleasure.

"It feels... so... good," I mumble breathlessly. "So fucking deep."

"You love it fast and hard like this, don't you?" he rumbles, gently massaging my clit between his thumb and forefinger. I let out a shriek, my legs quaking. Sal chuckles, a low, gravelly sound that vibrates through my body.

"Yes, yes, yes," I mutter, tightening my legs around his neck as he slams into my pussy.

"Such a filthy, good little girl," he snarls, squeezing my breast in one massive hand. He's playing me like a damn guitar, tweaking my body in all the right places, stroking me to climax.

"Come for me, baby," he purrs. "Give me more of that sweet honey."

He picks up the pace, fucking me faster while he rubs my tingling clit in a tight circle.

"Oh god. Oh my god, Sal!" I exclaim, my cunt gushing with another orgasm.

"Yes. Fuck, yes. Just like that. Good girl," Sal whispers. "You're so fucking beautiful."

He leans down over me, cradling my back with one powerful arm. I reach up for him, my hand brushing over the wound on his bicep, but he doesn't even wince. He kisses me deeply, his cock buried deep inside my pussy, pounding into my g-spot so hard it hurts.

"Open your eyes, Eva," he hisses. "I want to see the look in your eyes."

I obey, staring into his handsome face, locking with his dark eyes as he fucks me. Somehow, this is the most intimate part, just gazing at each other while he pounds me into oblivion. His eyes strike deep inside my soul, deeper than his cock, and it gives me a high I have never known before. He kisses me, swallowing my moans as I come again, my pussy clenching and contracting around his swollen shaft.

"Please," I murmur, licking my lips. "Come inside me, Sal. I want to feel you come in my pussy. I need it. Fill me up."

That's all the persuasion he needs. Gripping me tight, resting his forehead against mine, he thrusts into my pussy a few more times and then blows his hot, sticky seed deep inside me.

"Fuck! Eva!" he bellows, diving forward and kissing me hard, his tongue pushing into my mouth while he pumps me full of his come. I squeeze him tight, milking every last drop, my body shuddering with desire and exhaustion. We stay like this for a few minutes, both of us breathing raggedly, eyes locked on each other, while the afterglow settles down around us like a warm veil. He kisses me softly, affectionately, cradling my face in his hands like I'm a precious jewel, something he's afraid to let go of. Afraid to lose.

Finally, he breaks away, his cock sliding out and his come starting to drip from my pussy, mingled with my own juices. Now that it's over, I feel a rush of embarrassment come over me, confusion at how the hell this even happened. I was a virgin. I hardly know Sal. I've just had the most life-changing, mind-blowing experience of my life, and I have no idea how to react to it now that it's over. Sal hands me a roll of paper towels, helping me up to my feet. I'm wobbly, feeling disoriented and physically spent. There's a look of silent conflict on his face, too.

Both of us are lost now. Unsure how to proceed.

He steps forward and gently kisses me on the forehead, then grabs me a towel that's been hanging to dry draped over the back of a chair. "The shower in the bathroom next to your bedroom works well," he says. "If you want to get cleaned up."

I nod, biting my lip. "Yes. Um, thank you," I say, a little awkwardly. Wrapping the towel around myself out of sudden modesty, I hurry out of the kitchen and down the hall, my heart pounding away as I walk into the bathroom and lock the door behind me.

I turn on the shower, my mind racing in a million directions.

What the hell was that? How did this happen? What have we done?

Who is this man and how does he have this effect on me?

Where do we go from here?

SALVATORE

I awaken the next morning feeling more rested than I've felt in a lifetime.

When I shower, the hot water that runs down my body relaxes muscles that have never felt so good. Every part of my body is still glowing from last night.

It was easily the best sex I've ever had.

And it was with the virgin I found in a hole in the ground under my new house.

The strangeness of the situation isn't lost on me, and even as I wash my body off, I have a feeling it isn't lost on her either. I can usually hear her moving around the house early, poking around the place and getting into everything I've been doing.

She thinks she's sneaky, but I can always hear.

This morning, though, it's quiet outside. So quiet,

in fact, that when I finish my shower and get clothes on, I sneak to her room. The door is ajar.

When I look inside, I see her laying on the bed, sheets half-strewn across her, and she stares up at the ceiling with as conflicted a face as I carry in my heart. Even so, she looks breathtaking, even when she's just waking up.

I'm thinking about how I wish we'd spent the full night together when she turns her eyes to look at me. We make eye contact for the briefest of moments before I clear my throat.

"Breakfast," I say simply, and I move to the kitchen.

I'm moving too fast with her. What I did with her could easily have scared a woman away, let alone a virgin. I could have woken up, and she would be gone, run off to the cops to tell them all about the bunker, her kidnapper.

And me.

I shake my head. I can't let that happen. But she was still there, in bed, with that strange, far off expression in her face. Wondering what she should do.

Wondering why she shouldn't just run.

I figure she's been taking this time to get used to her freedom, but time is running out for her. The longer she holds off going to the cops, the more questions they'll have for her, and the more her motivations will be questioned.

Why did you stay with the strange man in the woods? What did he tell you his name was? Salvatore... No. The Angel of Death? We heard he'd been killed in a mob shootout. Tell me, Eva, is this what he looks like? What did he tell you about the man who kidnapped you?

I shake my head free of the thought. It can't come to that, and the fact that she stuck around is a good sign. I need her to stay until I figure out what to do with her. A lot is on the agenda today. I cook up fat sausages that crackle and split, eggs, and thick pieces of toast with butter. I hurriedly eat mine while it's still scalding-hot and leave a plate out for Eva.

By the time she pads into the kitchen, I'm already halfway through my morning coffee.

She's wearing one of the loose shirts I bought her and a pair of tight leggings. My eyes drink her in as she enters, and she notices. There's another moment of eye contact between us, so charged that I can feel the electricity. Blushing, she quickly lowers her eyes and goes for her plate to start wolfing the food down.

I have to ignore the quiet pride I feel in how ravenously she devours my food. I don't let myself linger there, though. Before she's even halfway through, I finish my coffee and head outside into the cold morning air.

Even as I trudge across the yard, I can feel her eyes on me from the window.

Just one word has been spoken between us this

morning, but I can feel her presence on me. The shower couldn't totally wash away her scent, and it hangs on me as I make my way to the woodline around the yard.

Carrying wire, cutters, and a few mouse traps with me, I set to crafting a few trip wire alarms between some of the bigger trees around the perimeter in the places that seem most likely for someone to walk through—including the spot I used to approach the property.

Thinking like a hunter gives me a unique advantage when I'm being hunted.

Grabbing the rest of my toolbox, I set about using the rest of the morning to rig the place into a true safe house. I change the locks on the front door, set up simple wooden bars at the edges of the windows to make them impossible to open, and I even set up metal grating in the chimney to block it off—not that the fireplace is in use anymore, but those are just the kinds of weaknesses I would keep an eye out for.

I install a strike-plate into the front and back door jambs in case I need to buy time for a sudden police raid or all-out attack on the house. They're not options I like to consider, but they're necessary.

How is she any safer here with you than out there, my mind chides me, and I narrow my eyes. It's a round-about way of reminding me that I'm lying to her. That every word I say about protecting *her* is about protecting *me*. If she leaves and calls the cops, I'm the one up shit creek.

Unless the Mafia thinks she means something to me. I stop at the thought, my heart pounding a bit heavier in my chest, and not just from the renovations. No, suddenly I realize that in protecting myself, I've put her in more danger.

Pull yourself out of it, man. No one's getting in here without a firefight, and you'll keep her safe.

I focus back on my work, and start installing a peephole for the front door when I hear the pattering of feet behind me. I look over my shoulder, but Eva is gone.

I frown.

We've been half-avoiding each other all morning, but I can tell that she wants to be around me as much as I want to be around her. If she's thinking anything like me, it's because we just don't know what to make of... everything last night.

It was incredible. Just thinking back to the way she felt in my lap makes me start to grow hard even while my thick hands work my power tools.

But was it right?

No, of course it was not. I am a killer, someone who takes lives and has abandoned his conscience long ago. She's a broken girl who has suffered so, so much in her young life. Her innocence should be protected.

But isn't it already gone?

I clench my jaw as I work. Maybe the tug of guilt in the back of my head is right, and I've already ruined her. She made the first move—she wants me. But like a demon of temptation, I led her down that road, egging her on the whole way.

I even came in her, for fuck's sake.

When I finish the peephole, I roll my shoulders and head outside.

Maybe some fresh air and exercise will clear my head, and I have something in mind that I've been holding off on for a while.

I head around back to the shed, that fateful building where I first found Eva. It truly looks like something from a slasher movie from the outside. I head in and look around at the ruins of the horror show.

When I'd first stepped in, I assumed this was just where that old man watched his dirty movies and got off on some odd fetishes. I had no idea it was so much more. Hell, I didn't even suspect that he would have *this* setup.

I walk to the hatch in the floor that leads down to the bunker. Paranoid old misers are fond of such things, usually claiming they want a place to hide when the apocalypse comes. That was probably what Geoffrey Mink told the people who built this dungeon.

Looking around at the tech, I confirm what I was

thinking: all this stuff is old. Ancient, by my standards. It all needs to go.

I do one last sweep around the horrific office, and I only find one thing I decide to hang onto—Mink's laptop. It was still open when I took over the property, so it has clearly seen recent use. I close the laptop and carry it inside.

I hear quick footsteps as soon as I get in, and I hold back a sigh.

Eva can't keep running from me as if she's afraid of me. Maybe she is, but that doesn't change the fact that we'll eventually have to talk about what happened.

But then another thought occurs to me. Smiling, I head off to my tools.

A few moments later, I knock on Eva's door, then push it open. She's sitting there on the bed, looking a little guiltily up at me as though she knows I'm going to confront her for something she did wrong.

Instead, I hold up the sledgehammer in my hand, and her eyes go wide.

"I have something for you," I say. "Get dressed."

"Are we going somewhere?" she asks, her eyes fluttering.

"Just outside," I say. "Don't dress too heavily."

Ten minutes later, Eva is trotting up behind me as I head to the shed. When she realizes where we're going, she stops dead in her tracks.

I look over my shoulder at her with a raised eyebrow, but she just stares at me.

"What?"

"Are we... what are we doing?" she asks, her eyes on the sledgehammer I hold in my hand.

I let out a laugh, shaking my head. The sound of it seems to take her off-guard.

"Trust me. You'll enjoy this."

Cautiously, she follows after me. I push the door open and lead her inside.

She visibly tenses at the sight of all the monitors. Some of them are still on, the haunting stillness of the empty bunker room still flickering on the screens.

This place will haunt her for the rest of her life.

But maybe I can make it a little better.

I snap her out of her trance by stepping forward, and she looks at me nervously.

Without a word, I smile and hand her the sledgehammer.

Her eyes widen, looking down at it and then up to me as if asking me to confirm what she's thinking.

"All yours," I say, taking a few steps back to the door.

She's stunned for a few more moments, then her beautiful lips start to spread into a smile, and that smile spreads into a grin.

Watching her small frame try to hold the sledge-hammer almost makes me laugh, and I cross my arms proudly as I watch her look around at all the machinery like a kid in a candy store.

"Be careful how you sling it around, it's easy to throw your back out," I warn her, but she just flashes a grin at me.

"I don't think I need a tutorial for this," she says, and with that, she throws her weight into a mighty swing at one of the big monitor screens.

It crumples with a satisfying crash of glass, plastic, and metal, and the giddy grin on Eva's face makes my heart feel like it's being pumped full of air, swelling with joy.

She swings it around to the next monitor, then brings it down to crash into one of the computer towers. Within a couple of minutes, she completely annihilates an entire table full of equipment, including the table itself.

I'd expect someone her size to run out of steam pretty fast, but the energy she picks up is incredible. Once one wall of cameras is smashed, she moves right into the next as if she'd just done a shot of espresso.

Every swing is full of enthusiasm and bloodlust.

"Yeah! Fuck you!" she shouts, her tiny voice so full of furious glee that it makes me laugh a little. She handles the sledgehammer beautifully, each swing bringing pounds and pounds of force onto whatever unfortunate equipment she's wrecking next.

When she takes a breather, setting the sledgehammer down and resting on the handle to breathe, I slip past her and open the hatch to the vault. She watches me curiously, but I say nothing as I go down there and into the bunker.

A few minutes later, I emerge, hauling the wooden wardrobe full of scantily-clad clothing her captor left for her.

Just like that, her tired face is refreshed all over again.

This little woman has a lot of rage in her. I can appreciate that.

"Don't need a breather?" I say as she readies her hammer again, then drives it full-force into the wood. This time, though, the hole it makes in it is a little less impressive than the destruction she inflicted on the computers.

"No!" she insists, panting, "I got this!"

She readies her hammer again, then lowers it, her breaths heavy.

"Well, okay, maybe I could use a quick break. Want in on this action?" she asks, grinning over at me, and I smile calmly as I take the sledgehammer in one big hand.

"Stand back," I say. She does, and I ready the hammer.

In one solid swing, I bring it over my head and down onto the wardrobe. The wood splinters and crumples like paper under my blow with a thunderous crash.

Eva gasps and nearly stumbles back, eyes wide at me, but the surprise quickly turns to laughter, and she claps her hands as she watches me pull back and swing again.

Her enthusiasm spurs me on.

With four more solid crashes, I reduce the wardrobe full of skimpy clothing to a pile of shredded cloth and wrecked wood.

The next hour goes by in the same fashion. Eva eventually goes back into the house to get us some water while I pull out pieces of furniture from the vault and haul it up to start wrecking. I eventually have to start dragging the ruins out of the shed when it becomes too much to fit into one place.

I plan to keep the shed up. Eva and I destroy most of the stuff that made up her prison, but I don't plan to destroy the bunker itself. There is still a year's worth of canned goods in there, and in case the heat turns up too high, it will be a good place to hole up. Literally.

Even our energy has its limits, though, and after a fair amount of time, I notice that Eva is really running out of steam. I plant the head of the hammer into the ground and rest my hands on it, watching her surveying the wreckage with tired satisfaction.

"How did that feel?"

"Good," she says without missing a beat. "Really good." She looks over at me, my ripped figure standing over the hammer still as a statue, and I see her blush before looking away. I smile.

"I'm glad," I say, and I nod to the house. "Let's rest."

We head inside, and as we enter the house, Eva's eyes fall on the laptop that I brought in. She furrows her eyebrows.

"That's new. Was it his, too?"

I nod, walking over to the thing on the table and opening it. He didn't even have a password lock on it. "Yes. I want to make sure there's nothing important on it before I hand it over to you."

I see that he has his emails open, and I slowly scroll through them as she smiles beside me.

"Don't suppose you have any explosives I could use on this thing?"

I smile and open my mouth to reply, but she leans forward suddenly, eyes wide.

"Wait," she asks, putting her hand on mine to stop me. "Let me see that."

She points to one of the emails.

"Can you check that one?"

I arch an eyebrow at her, then open it.

It's a short message, the latest in a short conversation. I can see the first line of each exchange, and I furrow my brow as I recognize what looks like someone reaching out to Mink to do a job.

A hit.

The last email is dated to about a month ago.

The money will be transferred as you requested. I expect the job to be done within a week so he has time to change his will back before he dies. We don't have time to waste with my father being sick. I want her gone entirely, and I don't care how you do it as long as it happens soon. She brought this on herself by turning up. Do this and you'll have a better retirement than you can imagine.

-B

The email was sent from blake@brightoncorp.com, a pathetically stupid and sloppy use of a company email.

It reads like some corporate idiot sloppily trying to get some loose end tied up, but when I look over at Eva, her eyes are shining with tears, and her mouth is hanging open at the screen.

"What is it?"

"That email..." she breathes, putting a hand over her mouth. She looks at me, red-rimmed eyes wide and fearful. "That email is talking about me!"

EVA

I stare at the email, eyes wide and mouth hanging open. This can't be real. This can't be happening. Somehow, this has got to be a cruel joke. A prank of some kind. Surely my own brother—well, half-brother—wouldn't do this to me. Hell, he hardly knows me! We met once. Briefly. And that was somehow enough for him to judge me by and decide I need to be eliminated?

Tears are burning in my eyes, my blood running cold.

"Eva," he says slowly. "Do you know this guy? This Blake Brighton?"

I nod, struggling to find the words I want to say. "I know him. Kind of."

"Kind of?" Sal presses gently, laying a hand on my shoulder. A hot, angry tear rolls down my cheek and drops down to stain my shoulder. "How do you *kind of* know him?"

"He's my brother," I murmur softly. The word 'brother' is bitter in my mouth.

It was a brief letter, cut straight to the point. He wants me gone. Not just disappeared, but dead. And he was willing to step down from his ivory tower and conspire with a lowlife like the man who kidnapped me to get the job done.

"Forgive me, Eva," Sal says, his heavy brow furrowed as he looks at me from over the email. "But I'm having trouble putting the pieces together here. I know we have both been operating under a sort of mutually hands-off approach."

I raise an eyebrow at him and a look of realization crosses his face.

"Not that hands-off," I comment in an undertone. Sal sighs.

"Yes, apart from that. What I mean is that we have been keeping secrets from each other. But this," he says, pointing to the email, "is serious. It is sloppily written, which indicates that the writer is careless, too full of himself to be cautious. He clearly has no experience ordering something like this, but he's so foolhardy and self-assured he isn't worried about being caught. Now, Eva, this is the difficult question: does this description sound like your brother?"

I bite my lip, thinking it over for a moment. If this is what I think it is, what it appears to be, then I am about to accuse my own half-brother of something very serious. Deadly serious. Do I really know him well enough to make such a heavy assumption about his character?

"Yes," I reply simply. "It sounds like him."

"Why would he do this?" Sal continues, folding his arms over his broad chest and looking very grim. "What reason would your brother have to threaten your life?"

"Are we sure that's what it is?" I mumble, wringing my hands. "I mean, could it be a joke? A really bad prank?"

Sal fixes me with a stern, questioning look. "I'll ask again: does *that* sound like something your brother would do? A prank? How old is this guy?"

"About a year younger than I am," I admit. "He's not a child."

"You said you didn't know him well. Can you be certain?"

"We didn't exactly grow up together," I confess. "Actually, we never even met each other until about a month ago."

Sal looks surprised for a moment, and then it seems to make sense to him.

"So, I take it you never had a healthy, functional family life either, then."

I shake my head, tucking my hair behind my ears, feeling a little ashamed. I never share information like this with anyone. Ever. I don't want their pity. I don't want people to look at me like I'm some fragile, wounded little animal. I want to be seen as strong and competent, not a broken little girl who never knew her father. That is a can of worms I keep very tightly sealed.

Sal starts pacing.

"So, tell me more."

I wince. "About what?" I ask, already knowing the answer.

"About your family," he replies matter-of-factly.

I groan and pull up a chair, sitting down. "I don't talk about this stuff with anyone," I tell him. "Hell, until about a month ago I never even thought about it myself."

"What happened a month ago?" he asks.

"Out of nowhere, my deadbeat father reached out to me. Sent me a letter with the same logo and heading as that email right there," I begin, pointing to the email. "Brighton Manufacturing. It's a really successful business in Rochester."

"Wait, you're telling me that you lived in the same city as your father, but the two of you never crossed paths?" Sal inquires, narrowing his eyes. "How is that possible?"

I nod. "Yep. I know. It sounds crazy. Rochester may not be a big city, but let's just say we existed in two totally separate circles. He's always been on one side of the railroad tracks and, well, I've always been on the other side."

"What do you mean?" Sal asks. "Elaborate."

"Do I really have to?" I groan, rolling my eyes. Sal doesn't relent.

"Yes. Eva, this is a death threat. This is a hit. Your brother apparently ordered your death. This is serious. I need as much information as you can give me."

"Why? What can you do to fix it?" I shoot back, waving my arms. I know I'm being difficult. I'm getting too defensive. None of this is Sal's fault. If anything, he's the one rescuing me from my own life. But when I feel cornered, I tend to strike out at whoever is closest. Which is yet another reason why I always keep to myself. I don't get hurt, and nobody else gets hurt either. But Sal is persistent, unruffled by my outburst.

He walks over and kneels in front of me, taking my hands into his bigger ones and looking at me with genuine concern. There's a soft patience in his enchanting dark eyes, and despite everything, it calms me.

"Eva, I don't know yet what I can do, but I can promise you that I will do whatever it takes to make this right. I refuse to let anyone harm you. Never again," he says sincerely, gazing into my eyes in a way that somehow relaxes me and makes my heart race at the same time. "But I won't know how to proceed until you give me a little more information, okay?"

I take a deep breath, summoning all my strength.

"Okay. But you have to understand: I have never told anyone about this. I don't talk about my past. It's—it's a little painful for me," I start off, blushing.

"That's alright. Take your time," Sal says gently, squeezing my hands. "How about you start with your father?"

"Ugh," I say, shuddering. It's a reflex to grimace at the mention of my dad. He hasn't exactly been a positive influence on my life. "I never knew him. My mom raised me."

"Did he know about you?" Sal asks. I wrinkle my nose. "I know. It's an awful question."

"He did," I admit. "He knew all about me. He knew my mother was pregnant. She told him. But what they had together—it was hardly more than a fling. A one-night stand, even."

"And so, when your mother told him she was pregnant with you, what did he do?"

I make a sound of annoyance. "He ignored her. Gave her the cold shoulder. He made it very, very clear that he was finished with her and wanted nothing to do with either of us."

"Why not?" he asks, frowning.

I can feel my cheeks going red with a combination of anger and embarrassment.

"Because that's just the kind of guy he is, Sal. My mom wasn't from his world, you know. My father was a rich, powerful man even back then before I was born. And my mom was like me, from the other side of town. I'm sure he probably would have been too embarrassed to even admit he'd slept with her. She was a waitress. They met while he was at the restaurant she worked in. My mother was a really beautiful woman. Even when she died, she was beautiful. He should have thanked his lucky stars that she was into a guy like him. He never knew how wonderful she was. I'm sure he never gave her a chance to prove it to him," I say bitterly.

"Your mother is…?"

"Yes. She died five years ago," I explain quickly, wanting to gloss over this part. "It's still hard to talk about."

"How did she die, if you don't mind my asking?" he says.

I look down at the floor. "She was in an accident. The whole time I was growing up, we could never afford a car. My mom used to take me with her on the bus. But when I was eighteen, she finally had saved up enough for a used car. Used, but new to her. Just a little four-door sedan, but she was so damn proud of it. Finally a car-owner," I say, smiling at the memory.

"What happened?" Sal presses softly.

I have to bite my lip to stop from crying. "She only had that car for a few months when she got into an accident. Wasn't even her fault. Some long-haul trucker was coming off a week-long stint. It was just after midnight. He was exhausted, apparently, falling asleep behind the wheel. My mother was leaving her night shift at the restaurant. There were hardly any other cars on the road, but it was February and the streets were all icy and slippery. My mom was a very careful driver. It was actually kind of annoying sometimes. She always drove a few miles under the speed limit. People used to honk at her all the time," I laugh faintly. Then I get serious again, remembering the accident. "I got a call at three in the morning from the police. Informing me that my mom was killed in an accident. The trucker didn't see her, went barreling through a red light and by the time he saw my mom, it was too late. He hit the brakes but the eighteen-wheeler went skidding over the ice and knocked my mom's car into a ravine."

"Good god," Sal swears, reaching up to touch my face. My tear rolls down his hand.

"Yeah. It was a swift death, they said. She probably felt a few moments of fear, and then nothing. She was killed instantly on impact."

"Small mercy," he says. "I'm so sorry, Eva. That's horrible."

"It was," I agree. Sniffling, I try to regain my composure. "Anyway. She was an amazing woman. She worked harder than anyone I've ever known, and no matter how difficult things were, how cruel people were, she never stopped believing that people are good at heart. She was so patient and kind. She was always telling me to have faith, that good things come to those who wait. But that's not true. Not in my experience. I guess I just can't be an optimist like she was."

"Well, it sounds like you've struggled to get by," Sal reasons. "I can see why you might feel less inclined to have faith."

"Exactly," I admit. "That's it."

"And so you've been alone for the past five years," he says.

I nod, looking away. I can't meet his eyes. I'm afraid I'll see something like pity there, and I can't bear it. "Pretty much. I can take care of myself."

"But you shouldn't have to," he interjects. I finally meet his gaze, and instead of pity, all I see is understanding. Compassion. "I've been alone for a long time too. It is a good way to guard your heart, but it comes at a great price."

"I suppose that's true," I murmur.

"So, tell me about your father and your brother," he says, steering me back on course. I frown, anger flushing my face for a second as I'm pulled from a pleasant moment into much more uncomfortable memories.

I shrug. "I don't know them. Not really. My father called me into his office to meet with him and some lawyers. Apparently, he's getting pretty old and he's feeling guilty in his old age. Guilty for ignoring me and my mom, pretending we never existed. So he called me there to assuage his guilt, I guess. It was a lot of legal jargon, stuff that's meant to be so complicated nobody can understand it. I tried to follow along, but I was a little overwhelmed."

"What was the gist?"

"He wanted to add me to his will, it seemed," I say. Sal's eyes go wide for a moment.

"And your brother was present for this meeting?"

"Yes. He just kind of stood over in the corner, frowning at me. Turning up his nose at me like I was some mangy dog instead of a human being," I describe. "I could tell from the second I laid eyes on him that he was a spoiled brat. Expensive, slightly tight suit to make him look bigger than he was. Frosted, spiked tips in his hair." I scoff. "Hard to believe we're related."

"He probably never expected your father to include you in the will," Sal says. It dawns on me what he's implying, and I shake my head.

"No. He has nothing to worry about. My father may have included me in the will out of a guilty conscience, but he's still a scumbag. He would never leave me anything of note. I'm sure my inclusion was just a formality."

"Well, whether that's true or not, your brother might not know that," Sal explains, standing up and pacing again. "He's spoiled, like you said. Used to getting everything he wants without a fight. It would be a huge blow to his ego for your father to suddenly include you. Even the sheer idea of having to share the fortune with you would infuriate him. And men like him are petulant. Reckless. They don't think things through. I have known many men like your brother. They attack first, apologize later. Or never."

"I'm willing to bet on 'never,'" I add.

"Me, too," Sal agrees. "Eva, this man may not be smart, but he is dangerous. Excessive wealth and a lack of conscience is a deadly combination. But we do have one advantage."

I frown, confused. "And what is that?"

Sal gives me a wry smile. "Blake Brighton thinks you are dead."

"So what?" I ask, shrugging.

"He assumes you're out of the picture. No longer a threat. That means that as long as you lay low and stay hidden, he'll have no reason to be on his guard. Emboldened by his perceived success, he will continue to make reckless mistakes. He'll think he got away with it, and that is exactly what we want him to think."

"So I guess it's a good thing I've been hiding out here," I murmur. Once more, I wonder if fate is at play. Some divine force trying to protect me from dangers I don't even know are there.

And it turns out Sal was right. It wasn't safe for me out there.

"Yes. It is. And you'll have to keep hidden. I will do what I have to. You've given me some very helpful information. But I need to know more, to find out exactly who we are dealing with."

"And do what about it, exactly?" I ask.

Sal looks at me with those dark eyes blazing. "Your brother has made the first move, but now it's our turn to play the game."

"*A*re you sure breaking and entering is the *first* step in this game?" Eva asks me as I pull my car to a stop under a shady tree near a large, empty parking lot under a looming office building.

"Yes," I say curtly, and I reach behind the seat to pick up a black bag and set it in my lap. "Gathering intel is the first step to any job. You can't accuse him of anything unless we have information on our side. Especially information he doesn't think you have."

Eva has a good memory. She directed me to the Brighton Corp offices from her sole visit here. Convincing her that it was necessary to come here after hours was only easy because I sprung it on her quickly, and that was intentional—I didn't want to give her enough time to backpedal.

"He must not even know I'm alive," she says, her voice sounding a little distant, and I look over to her.

I set a hand on her leg and give her thigh a gentle squeeze, and she smiles at me.

"We'll use that to our advantage," I say. "If he thinks you're dead, he thinks all his problems are gone. His guard is down."

"Right," she says, taking a deep breath and looking up at the looming tower in front of us. "And that is why... we're... breaking... into his office." She says the words as if she can't believe she's saying them.

I smile. It's been a while since working with someone so inexperienced.

"I'm not killing anyone," I say.

"The fact that you have to clarify that does *not* help," she says, and I roll my eyes. I take out a headpiece from the bag and hand it to her.

"Put this on your ear. It will let us communicate. If something goes wrong down here, tell me."

"Goes wrong?" she asks, her eyes wide.

"If someone gives you trouble for being parked here," I explain, "or anything else."

She takes a breath, eyes wide, and nods. "Right. Sure. I'll just explain to the cops that I'm here investigating my kidnapping by breaking into a CEO's office."

"Perfect," I say with a sarcastic grin.

"So I'll be honest," she says, looking up and down at my all-black outfit, "it *looks* like you know what you're doing, but, I mean, do you?" Her question isn't a challenge—I know she's just prying to know more about me. What we're doing tonight is certainly enough to raise some questions.

"Yes," I say simply, and before she can say anything further, I get out of the car and make my way toward the building.

"Can you hear me?" I say a few steps later into my headpiece.

"Um. Yeah," comes her voice in my ear.

"Good," I say, "I'm going in."

I have only one gun and one knife in my clothes. I'm not expecting a firefight, but if there is one, I'm not defenseless.

Getting low to the ground, I move up to the back of the building and crouch behind an elevated ramp by one of the fire exits. I reach into my jacket and take out a black jack—a small leather rod with hard metal inside.

My eyes go up to the floodlights above the doors, and I follow the wires down to a small metal box not far from where I'm hiding. I move over to it, take out a pair of wire cutters, and with a quick motion, the lights go out.

Now, all I have to do is wait.

Fortunately, it doesn't take long. The fire door opens, and one of the security guards walks out. He's a tall, stocky man, and I hear him grumbling about a rat problem as he makes his way down the ramp.

I intercept him.

Jumping up on the railing, I grab him by the scruff of his collar and hit him over the back of the head with my black jack. He doesn't even have time to shout before he goes unconscious.

In the darkness, I drag him behind a hedge and take his hat, overshirt, and badge. That's all I need for the cameras inside.

Keeping my head down, I start making my way up the stairs of the fire escape.

Most office buildings at least leave their stairways mostly barren, but even the fire escape route in this office looks fancy, all a modern, sleek, black design with the occasional piece of art hanging on the wall.

I take the stairs up as high as I possibly can. If Blake Brighton keeps his office here, it'll be at the top of the building.

"How're things going in there?" I hear a cautious voice say over my earpiece after some time of climbing.

"Getting a workout," I whisper back. "All clear out there?"

"I saw some movement by the building a while ago," she says.

"That was me," I say. "If you see something move there again, let me know."

"Um... roger?" she says, and I crack a smile.

Finally, I get to the top floor and peer through the window to the main hallway. The light of a guard's flashlight is shining on the walls for a few moments, but soon, he turns it away and walks the opposite direction. I take care not to make noise while opening the door, and I slip in.

Blake's office is easy to locate. There's an opening to a lobby with tiled floor and large plants decorating it, and a heavy door stands on the opposite end of the room.

There's an empty receptionist's desk next to it.

I make my way over to it, carrying myself as if I'm a regular security guard who belongs there. I know there are at least four camera angles on me.

Fortunately, I'll never be seen here again after tonight.

At the receptionist's desk, I hold my stolen badge over a little glass scanner, and it beeps softly. I press the button under it, and I hear the door to the main office to my left click open. I look up as I hear footsteps coming my way, and I slip into the office hurriedly.

The space inside is large and lavish. If I were a CEO, I wouldn't mind a place like it. Black floors and ceilings, and my guess is the lights are a dull white. The big black desk in the middle of the room is curved and covered by papers, folders, and a few computer monitors. A few inconspicuous plants line the walls, and over them hang pieces of modern art.

I make my way to the desk and take out a small thumb drive from my pocket. Rather than dig through all the information by hand, I plan to take it all home and sort through it later, so to speak. His personal laptop is easy to spot, standing out from the rest of the office stylistically. What's more, it's still open.

I stick the thumb drive in, and the screen flickers on to show a personal email open. Blake is clearly not used to having to be smart in his work.

Still, I don't touch anything—instead, the program I have on my thumb drive does the work of downloading everything I need for me.

Three minutes into the download, I hear the door click.

My heart doesn't stop, and my face doesn't go pale—I just act.

I drop to my knees and cram myself under the desk, and I remain perfectly still as the door swings open, and I hear footsteps entering the room. They walk slowly, and I see the light of a flashlight pass overhead.

There's silence for a few seconds before I hear a voice.

"... Rob? You in here again? Told you your ass is fired if I catch you reading HR emails again."

I nearly hold my breath as the guard waits for an answer, coming closer. His legs appear in front of me.

My hand is on my gun.

All he has to do is look down, and our eyes will meet.

I hold my breath and grip the pistol, finger sliding to the trigger.

The guard's legs turn.

He walks back out the door, muttering to himself as the door slams shut behind him. I let out a breath, removing my hand from the gun and coming out of the desk.

The thumb drive has finished its work. I take the little piece of plastic full of terabytes of information, and I move to the door to make my escape.

* * *

ON THE DRIVE HOME, Eva has said little to me. She was stunned when I got into the car as I left, having abandoned the guard's items with the unconscious man. I just handed her the thumb drive and took off.

Finally, as we're getting close to the driveway to the safe house, she takes in a breath and speaks.

"What *was* that?"

"A break-in," I say simply.

"You know what I mean," she says, her voice a little less patient than usual.

I arch an eyebrow at her.

She throws up her hands, rolling her eyes, and stammers a little. "You're like, six and a half feet tall, wear all black, hardly say a word, and you just broke into one of the richest corporate offices in the *state* like you were stopping for dinner at a fast food place."

"I don't eat fast food."

She lets out an exasperated sigh as we pull up to the house, and I get out of the car. I start to make my way casually to the house, but she jogs around the car to catch up to me, those brilliant blue eyes looking up at me defiantly.

"The more you shut me down, the more I'm going to ask, you know," she says. "Who *are* you? I'm glad you found me, and I can't believe I'm lucky enough that you're willing to help me, but..."

I stop in my tracks, frowning down at her in silence for a few long moments. Her resolve doesn't melt away. We just stare at each other, tense, searching each other's eyes.

Finally, I break the silence, speaking slowly, each deep syllable pronounced carefully.

"I'm a man who bought a safe house, doesn't go into town, wants you to stay out of sight, and was able to get the information you need to save your life." I pause, letting that all sink in before continuing. "If that makes you nervous, perhaps you should think twice before prying too far into my life."

I walk past her, nodding for her to follow me into the house.

"It's late, you should get to bed," I say once we're inside. She follows me silently, but her searching eyes are on me—I can tell she's hardly swayed by my words. That's new.

"What are you going to do?" she asks.

"More work on the house," I lie. "I don't want to fall behind my schedule. I like to keep things timely."

"At night?"

"If need be," I say. We stare at each other for another few seconds before she turns on her heel and heads down the hallway, her feet stomping a little louder than necessary.

I roll my eyes and shake my head as I head outside.

She was right, of course. It would be stupid to do any kind of work in the darkness. But there is one thing that I need to take care of before I move ahead with the renovations, especially since there's another set of eyes and hands prying around the house now.

I make my way down to the freezer after I hear Eva's door close.

I open the lid and look down at the frozen remains of Geoffrey Mink.

Loading them into a sack, I make my way back out to the yard and head to the shed. There's no quiet way of doing what I'm about to do, but out here in the woods where manual labor and wood-working is constantly happening, there's much less risk involved than there would be anywhere else.

I have a wood chipper hooked up around the side of the shed.

Eva thinks I'm doing a little construction, so the noise shouldn't worry her too much. I open the sack and look over the pieces of the horrible, evil old man, frozen solid. It's a grizzly thing, disposing of a body, but I take pleasure in knowing that it means this man will never be able to hurt anyone ever again.

I put on some hearing protection, turn the wood chipper on, and hear the hellish noise it makes, muffled to my ears.

I pick up the first piece of Mink and slowly feed it into the machine.

As I work, my thoughts are distracted by Eva. Having her around is a definite risk, and I can tell that she's smart. I'm sure she's figured a few things out about who I am and what I do, but I wonder how deep her curiosity will take her.

More importantly, I worry what she will do when she finds out who I really am.

The body parts I feed into the machine come out messily on the other side, but this will ensure Mink's body is never a problem for me. They're spraying out onto some of the wreckage we destroyed earlier, too, which we'll burn as ordinary garbage later. Two birds, one stone, as long as I can keep the smoke under control.

With all that out of the way, maybe I can give this broken girl something close to a cozy home. And maybe then, between that and the strange and interesting turn of events her own life has taken, she'll forget all about prying into me.

Wishful thinking, I tell myself with a smile.

But as I finish the dark deed and turn the wood chipper off to make sure everything is taken care of, something feels off. The hairs on the back of my neck stand on end.

I feel watched.

I turn my head toward the house, and for the first time tonight, what I see makes my heart skip a beat.

Eva's white face is watching me from the window.

She saw everything.

EVA

"What the hell?" My heart pounds mercilessly in my chest.

Sal has turned around, his eyes locking on me. His expression hardens and he starts running toward the house. I let out a little shriek of fear and bolt from the window, tripping over a box of tools and skidding across the floor. My eyes dart around, desperately searching for a place to hide. Where the hell do I go? What do I do? There's nowhere to hide where he won't find me!

And besides, why am I even bothering to hide?

Didn't Sal make it abundantly clear that he would protect me? Keep me safe from harm? Doesn't that include keeping me safe from himself?

The back door opens with a click and Sal comes lumbering in, snowflakes scattered over his clothing and his dark hair. I make a reflexive move as though to try and dart away from him, but I stop myself. Something in his expression stops me in my tracks. The look on his face is one of mingled worry and… hurt, perhaps? Like it causes him physical pain to see me backing away from him. Like it's breaking his heart that I'm frightened of him.

But that's the thing. I'm not frightened of him. I know I should be. Every shred of logic in my brain urges me to listen to it, to abide the rules. I just caught Sal doing something blatantly horrific, didn't I? Wasn't that a body he was destroying? Evidence? Evidence of some hideous, gritty crime that should shake me to my core?

In place of fear, I'm… intrigued. Drawn to him by the same magnetic force that has sparked between us since the first time we set eyes on each other. That little voice in the dark corner of my mind whispers again: *I trust him*. He won't hurt me. Whoever it was that crossed him so violently as to deserve death must have earned it, because Sal is not a cruel man. A dangerous man, sure. A mysterious, dark figure whose past is shrouded in shadow, whose intentions and motivations are hidden from me? Yes. All of this is true.

And yet, I can't drag myself away from him. At my own peril, I walk toward him. Toward the darkness that threatens to swallow me whole. I step up to face the shadows with my heart open and my eyes watching, yearning to understand.

"I don't want to lie to you," Sal says gravely.

"Then don't," I reply defiantly, refusing to break eye contact. To his credit, he doesn't even try to look away. He doesn't shy away from the inevitable questions. He knows full well he's been caught and there's no going back, no ducking out of this. Not now. Not with me.

"What you just saw... I never wanted you to see any of that," he begins, haltingly.

"Well, I could have assumed that," I respond, folding my arms over my chest. "I knew you were dangerous from the moment I saw you. I tried to deny it to myself, but I know it's true. You wouldn't tell me who you are, what you do. You're not a builder. You're not a cop. So what are you, Sal? Who the hell are you?"

He sighs. "Your first impression was correct. I am dangerous. But not to you. Never to you. Eva, you have to understand that I would never hurt you. I couldn't."

"Answer the question," I press him, refusing to concede an inch.

His jaw tightens as he looks down at me, those dark eyes shining. "There is a reason I so quickly surmised the contents of that email your brother sent."

"Explain," I prompt.

"I have dealt with many men who wanted the same thing Blake Brighton asks for in that letter. I have carried out such orders myself," he says slowly. At first, I'm confused.

Frowning, I ask, "What do you mean? What orders?"

"Eva, your brother wants you dead. Normally, when someone wants someone else dead, they turn to someone like me for help," Sal explains, his tone flat and unaffected.

My heart skips a beat.

"What are you talking about?" I mutter, shaking my head in disbelief. "You can't be— you don't mean that—"

"Yes. Whatever you're thinking, it is probably true," he says softly.

I scoff, looking at him sideways. "You're fucking with me, right?"

He shakes his head slowly, not a hint of humor on his face. "No."

"You're not really a—a hit man, right? Is that what you're called? That's not possible. That's not a real thing," I ramble, falling into denial. "There's no way."

"There is a way. It's true. You guessed correctly," he answers coolly.

"So your job is to kill people like me for a living?" I ask flat out.

Again, a flicker of pain crosses his face. "No. Not people like you. Bad people."

"Bad people," I repeat, still in shock. "I think normally we rely on the criminal justice system to punish the bad people, Sal."

He takes a step forward. "The system fails. Justice is not always served."

"Yeah, so the proper answer is to take matters into your own hands? Really?" I ask venomously. "That's fucked up, Sal."

"I admitted that I'm a dangerous man. What I do for a living— what I used to do— is dangerous. Most would probably consider it immoral, I suppose."

"You suppose? Sal, you're a contract killer! The guy who kidnapped me, the guy Blake hired, *he* didn't even kill me! Is that why you're here? To finish the job?" I burst out.

Sal steps up and grasps my shoulders in his huge hands. I don't shy away, standing my ground as I gaze up at him. I know I'm doing it again: being too defensive. Too sharp. But Sal doesn't turn away from me. He stays. Despite my cruel words. Despite everything, he is patient.

"Eva, if I had wanted to kill you, you would already be dead," he says calmly.

"Oh, and that's supposed to comfort me?" I shoot back.

"No. It's supposed to inform you," he continues.

"Listen to me, Eva. That body— that filth you saw me disposing of out there— that is the man who brought you here. He was a bad person, Eva. A very bad man. He was hired to kill you, and believe me, he would have. But only after holding you hostage and torturing you. Watching you. Probably starving you. He has a reputation. Some consider it a reputation built entirely on whispers and rumors but I know the truth. It's all correct. He was a menace to society. He hurt people. Women, young children. He was lecherous and sadistic and he would have made you his next victim. He loved to toy with his victims before killing them. He liked to watch the joy, the humanity disappear before his very eyes, and only then would he release his victim with the gift of death."

I'm stunned into silence by the violence of his imagery. He goes on.

"That man— Geoffrey Mink, he was called— he would have done terrible things to you, Eva. Much worse things than he had done already. Your brother hired him no doubt because he was somehow aware of Mink's dwindling connections to the mafia."

"The mafia?" I repeat incredulously.

"Yes," Sal says, nodding. "That is how I knew Mink, too."

"Because you're..." I trail off, my stomach turning.

"Involved with the mafia, as well, yes," he admits readily. "And that is why I am in hiding just like you are. I betrayed the men I work for. I have made some very difficult, regrettable choices in my life, but I do not regret the path that led me here to you."

"And what path was that?" I ask, barely above a whisper.

"I used to follow orders without question. I was brought into the mafia at a young age. That's how they prefer their men. Young, with no better prospects. I was one of them, but I rose through the ranks quickly. I did what I had to do, and I questioned it as little as I could bear. I convinced myself I was killing bad people. And for the most part, I was. Until I realized that some of the worst men, the most deserving of death, were my superiors. The very men who brought me into the fold, who taught me everything I know. They were doing terrible things."

"Like what?" I ask, horrified.

Sal sighs. "Using drugs to convince increasingly young people to join their ranks. These recruiters for the mafia, they would prey upon high school students. Give them drugs, talk to them, pretend to listen to them and bond with them. All to trick them into trusting the mafia, thinking of us as family. Once these kids are addicted to drugs, the mafia pulls the rug out from underneath them and impresses them into service. It's worse than blackmail. They enslave every cell in these kids' bodies. It's disgusting."

"And you… did you do this, too?" I ask, afraid of

the answer. But Sal gives me a pained, offended look. He takes my hands in his.

"No. I would never do that. These men were recruiting children as young as fourteen, Eva. I could never do that to a kid. It's unforgivable. The young men were forced into service as thugs, killers. And the young girls were taken advantage of," he explains, disgust in his voice.

"Oh my god," I murmur.

"Yes. Once I discovered their methods, I knew what I had to do."

"They were bad people," I mumble.

He nods. "Very bad people."

"You killed them," I breathe.

"Yes. All of them. And I knew my transgression would not be forgiven. I needed someplace to run in the wake of my crime," he says.

"So you came here."

"I came here. I found out through some sleuthing that this place was under control of Geoffrey Mink, a man so vile that even the mafia pushed him out. And he was massively in debt. The safe house— this safe house— used to be a haven for mafiosos on the lam, but Mink was using it as a base camp for his own individual exploits. Such as you."

"Did you really buy this place under foreclosure?"

"Yes. A few of his checks went missing, cashed, but not to the bank. He never even knew it was up for foreclosure. Every dime he had to his name would have went to keeping this place off the market."

"And when you got here…"

"I killed Mink," he says calmly.

"And you saved me," I add, my heart nearly in my throat.

"Yes. I did not expect to find you here. I didn't plan for anyone else to be involved in my plan. But I don't regret anything I have done. And I did not lie to you when I said that I would protect you, Eva. I will protect you. From anyone who would dream of hurting you. I killed Mink and I would kill him a thousand times to protect you," he says. "And if your brother wants to hurt you, then he is my enemy. I will stop at nothing to keep you safe. That much I promise you."

I sit down on the dusty couch. It takes me several minutes of silence for everything to sink in, to make sense of this. But Sal stands by patiently. Waiting. Watching.

Finally, I speak.

"This is why you said it wasn't safe for me to go to the cops."

He nods, looking at me seriously. "I didn't want to question why you didn't want to go to them. I just was grateful for a small miracle. Until I could find out how to keep you safe and out of this mess.

"If I went to them, I would have told them about you. About how you saved me."

"And by the time you made your way back here, there wouldn't have been a trace left of me."

I frown at the thought.

"It would have been easier for you to kill me. No one knew I was down there."

Salvatore shakes his head, his face wincing in pain.

"No women. No kids. I don't have many morals, but those two things have gotten me through my life to this point. They don't ask for the mafia's wars."

"Do you understand why I stayed?"

He paused, looking at me seriously, surprised by the question.

"No, Eva. I do not understand why you wouldn't want to run all the way back to the police station, to your life, to everything that monster stole from you. I was just glad for it."

"I went to the police before. It was... a similar situation, I guess, in some ways. But it couldn't have been more different. It was just a date. I went back to his place, but that was when something in him changed."

Sal's lip twitches, knowingly.

"Yea. I got out, and he never... he didn't really do anything. But I was scared, and I thought if he did it to me, how many other girls was he doing it to? And what did he get away with. It made me sick. So even though I was safe, and he only scared me, I went to the police. Do you know what they did?"

Sal took in a deep breath, nodding as he moved his hand to cup my jaw, staring at me seriously. "Yes, I know what the pigs did. They said it was no big deal. That you were overreacting, and that your instincts and concern was misguided."

"Basically. They made me feel like it was all my fault, like I deserved it for going home with him. So when you saved me... I didn't want to face anyone. I didn't want to have to explain what happened, and hear all my worst thoughts put into words. I feel like an idiot being caught by... that monster," I say, refusing to use his name. "But now I know it really wasn't my fault. I wasn't just some easy target. I was a *paid* target."

"It was never your fault, even if you were an easy target. No one would ever want to be taken like that, do you understand?"

I stare up at him, tears flickering in my eyes. I've never told anyone any of this before, and to hear the fierceness in his voice makes my heart swell.

"I'm glad I stayed. It was the right choice. And I'm glad you were the one who found me."

A faint smile flickers over Sal's mouth.

"But if I'm going to stay safe, I need more than just you to protect me. I want to protect myself. I need to toughen up."

"What do you need?" Sal asks dutifully.

"You have a gun, I presume?" I ask. He nods and walks into the kitchen. I get up and follow him, still slightly dazed by all this new information. He opens a drawer and takes out a gun and a cartridge of bullets, holding them up for me to see. I nod.

"Of course you do," I murmur. "Okay. Here is what I need. Teach me how to use that."

Sal cocks his head to one side. "Right now?"

"Yes. Right now. No time like the present."

"Are you sure? You've just gotten a lot of info to process, maybe you should wait—"

"No," I protest, stepping closer. "Sal, I need this. Please. The world is darker and scarier than even I imagined, and that's saying something. So, yes. I need to learn how to shoot. Right now, right here. And you're going to teach me."

Sal sizes me up for a moment as though he expects me to take it back, but I don't. He takes me by the hand.

"Okay. In that case, let's step outside."

To his credit, he jumps right into a detailed explanation of how to handle, load, point, and fire a gun. He takes me in his arms, placing his hands over mine, helping me learn to judge distance and aim. We take hours with no break. Sal explains everything in close detail, with the relaxed, determined disposition of a seasoned professional. Like he's just explaining how to casually replace a light bulb or something. And I appreciate that. The last thing I need right now is for him to make a big deal out of this. If I am going to face up to my opponent, my own long lost half-brother, then I need to take this seriously. This is life or death, literally.

"Aim true and shoot," Sal says softly into my ear.

My heart is pounding. I have never fired a gun in my life. Never even touched a gun or seen one in person until now. I have no idea if I can pull this off or not, but Sal seems to have full faith in my abilities. That alone is enough to give me the confidence to pull the trigger.

The gun fires, jolting my entire body as the bullet goes flying and strikes the knobbly hole of a tree. The exact part of the tree I was aiming for. I'm so elated and exhilarated by the success that I nearly drop the gun. I let out a shriek of surprise and pride and turn back to Sal, who's grinning. He takes the gun from me and sets it down gently.

"That was fantastic," he says. "Spot on."

"I can't believe I did that!" I exclaim. "I really did it!"

"You did. I'm so proud of you. I've never met a girl like you before, Eva. Never in my life. You're not the scared little girl Geoffrey Mink probably thought you were. You're not a victim. You're a survivor. You're a badass," he compliments me, and I can tell every single word is purely genuine.

The thrill of firing a perfect shot, combined with the rush of wild emotions I've been experiencing for the past several hours bubble over and I throw my arms around Sal, jumping up into his arms. He catches me easily and kisses me, that familiar fire sparking and burning between us, threatening to consume us both if we aren't careful.

I know I should back away from the flame, but as he kisses me deeply, his hands tangling in my hair and stroking my face, I just can't. If I have to burn, I'll burn.

SALVATORE

The spark between us isn't just threatening to light up. It has already been fanned into a flame, and I think both of us know there's nothing we can do to stop it. The burning sun starts to rise behind us, lighting up the trees and making her look like an ethereal beauty.

I kiss her again. And again. And again, and our faces stay together as I walk us back toward the house. My arms hold her up as if she weighs nothing, and she puts her hands around the back of my head to pull herself up toward me and kiss me harder, letting out tongues flirt with each other between our lips.

I get past the door, but I only get as far as the couch before I stop to sit down with her, squeezing her, feeling her up. I'm full of greed and hunger, and all I want is to take more and more of her for myself.

Her blood is hot and full of need, despite all the innocence she's held onto for so long. She moans softly as I bring my mouth below her jaw and suck on the side of her neck. My teeth touch her skin, and I want to sink them into it. I nip her and breathe hot air on her, soft groaning from my chest getting her all the more excited.

I pull her shirt off before she has a chance to realize what I'm doing. My strong hands rip it away and toss it to the floor, and I squeeze her breast through the bra, thumb rolling over the soft fabric. I like how it teases me with what's underneath.

Her hands go to my shirt, tugging at it, pleading with me to make it go away as well. She leans back on my lap to let me do just that, and the next moment, I'm bare chested before her.

She gazes on me with pure desire.

Her hands go to my pecs, soft hands running down them and over my nipples until she lets herself press her face to my chest. She listens to my strong, heavy heartbeat while gently thrusting her hips forward against my lap.

I can feel her heat.

Her nails dig into my sides and run down them. Every muscle I have, every inch of my hardened body, she worships.

Her lips press against my pecs, and her hands go up to my shoulders to feel the muscles that run from my neck to my biceps. She squeezes, scratches, kisses, anything she can do to feel more of me.

I've had women hanging on me before, but none have been so thoughtful as Eva. She hungers for me, everything I have to give and more.

I squeeze her hips and pull her closer into me, just to show how much control I have over her body, even as she enjoys everything I have to offer. While she basks my body with attention, I unhook her bra, then push her back just enough to slide it off and toss it to the floor.

I put my hands behind her back and run a finger down her spine to make her arch her back for me and present herself completely and utterly, breasts bare and tempting me. Just as she kissed my chest, I kiss her breasts, and my tongue rolls out to taste her. I suck her breasts gently at first, but I get more aggressive when I get that feeling of her stiff neediness in my mouth.

My tongue flicks her nipples with its tip, swirling around the areolas, memorizing every detail of her body and how it feels. My cock is growing stiffer by the second as I feel her against my mouth. My hot breath washes over her nipples, but that doesn't keep them from getting stiff as if we were in the cold air outside.

My hands wrap around her waist and squeeze her harder, my body aching for her. But I'm going to deny myself just a little longer. I pick her up, and she whimpers as my mouth leaves her breasts, hands clawing for me a little, but she realizes that I'm turning her around, and she squirms around to make it happen.

I sit her on my lap facing away from me, and as soon as her ass is on my lap, she starts pushing it back into me, turning her head to look at me with lidded eyes.

"Fuck, Eva," I groan as I feel the soft give of her ass cheeks pushing through our clothes against my thick, ribbed cock. "Every time I see you, I want to bend you over the kitchen table again."

"Do you know how much I've dreamed about that night over and over again?" she says, her voice a whimper that makes my cock twitch.

I slide my finger around the waist of her pants until it reaches the front, and without more warning, I slip it under the fabrics to search out her pussy.

She gasps when the tip of my thick finger touches those hot, wet folds, and I rub them gently, feeling how ready she is for me.

"I'm going to give you something to dream about," I whisper into her ear in a husky tone.

Her mouth hangs open and her hair spills over my chest as she leans her head back and pushes her hips up into my touch.

I don't make it that easy for her, though.

Using my other hand, I hold her waist close to me, restraining her, pinning her to my hips while I finger her. My hand clenches around her possessively.

She squirms in my grasp and whimpers.

The tip of my finger touches that sensitive, swollen nub of her clit, and I start rubbing it gently, electrifying her pussy with the smallest movement. I rub my finger in small circles, taking in the rhythm of the way her folds slide around my finger.

She wants to wiggle away from my touch, but I hold her tightly in place. The sensitive touch I'm giving her is driving her wild and getting her wetter by the second. She puts her hands on my thighs and tries to dig them into the denim, sliding her ass back and forth as much as my snug grip allows.

I put my teeth on her neck again, gently brushing the sensitive skin, so very close to biting into her while I tease her clit. She starts pushing her hips up harder despite my hold on her. When I don't let her go, she whimpers.

The sound is like music to my ears.

"Come for me," I order her as my finger moves faster and faster around her clit, speeding up her own rhythm until I control it completely. Her breaths are short and desperate, and I can see the blush on her face as she gets closer and closer to the edge.

I feel her start to tighten and writhe in my grasp, but I never let her go, never relent, never slow down in my endless circles on her clit.

She lets out a sharp gasp when she comes, and I feel my finger wetter than ever.

I hold onto her through the orgasm, digging my finger into her and feeling every part of her I can reach as I guide her through the orgasm.

When it starts to come to an end, I stand up and toss her on the couch, unbuttoning my pants and letting my cock spring free.

I pull her pants down her hips, and she wiggles to get them just to her knees. I don't bother pulling them the rest of the way off or getting my pants off either. I want her.

Now.

For just a moment, I hold her hips in my hands, gazing at her glistening pussy and her ass cheeks, and I look past that to see her desperate, hungry face panting at me.

"Please, Sal," she gasps, "I... I want to feel you!"

My body has known her for so little time, but it hungers for her as if it's had her every night for years.

I seize her hips and spear her with my cock, hard and fast.

She gasps as I enter her, and this time, there's no going slow and steady, no sensual ease. I want to fuck her, hard and fast, and that's exactly what I'm going to do.

She's on the couch, topless, her pants halfway down her legs, and my cock is stuffed inside her, thick and throbbing with each buck of my hips. I start rutting into her with a powerful, energetic pace that's as precise as it is relentless.

With every thrust, her whole body shakes, and me holding onto her is the only thing that keeps her from getting run off the couch. My grip on her is as tight as it was when I was fingering her.

It's like I have an animalistic drive to hammer into her, something primal in me that makes it feel so sweet and right at the same time that each thrust makes my blood run hotter.

My body is near perfection. I have arms that have killed men twice as strong as me. But every inch of those muscles are in fire with lust for Eva, this broken girl impaled on my cock.

She's sweet and tight. My cock glides through her insides and grinds against everything, absolutely everything. There's nothing inside her that I can't claim, and I prove it to her.

I twist her hips to the left as I fuck her, then right, and each new angle lets me feel more of her, and I feel as her legs squirm and struggle in my grasp. She's utterly mine, and that fact makes me grow harder and stiffer than ever.

My balls are heavy and swollen with desire. I need to empty myself into her. I want to. Every muscle in my body wants it. But the more I ache for her, the sweeter it feels, the better each thrust is in her.

And as she gets tight and screams again, I know it's better for her, too. The force of her orgasm is almost enough to knock me over the edge of my own pleasure, but my control over my body *and* hers is absolute.

My cock is so hard that I feel like I could hold her up with it and nothing else. After her orgasm dies down, I pull out of her and slap her ass with a sharp crack that resonates in the room.

"On your knees," I order her, and she obeys like she was trained for it.

I grab her ass before she's even in position, and I thrust into her again, immediately hitting her g-spot and focusing all my attention there, pounding into her over and over again. I think about that first time we spent together, the look in her eyes and the sound of her voice when she asked to suck my cock.

It's enough to make me dizzy as I rut into her.

But that doesn't stop me. Nothing could, right now. Over and over again, my hips smack against her ass while my heavy, needy balls swing under her, and I hear moans of pleasure coming from her lips with each thrust. Soon, she grabs one of the cushions on the couch and digs her nails and her teeth into it, both to keep her stable and to give her something to bite into as I feel her getting tight around me again.

When the orgasm hits her, she screams into the cushion, absolutely letting loose all her inhibitions. The shuddering I feel in her body tells me just how good it feels, how complete and absolute the orgasm is for her.

And with that, I release myself.

My hips start bucking into her in less of a precise, machine-like pistoning and more of just a wild attack, an endless onslaught of force that sends me spiraling over the edge of my own control.

My hands have never lessened their grip on her hips, and even now, they don't. Even as I thrust wildly into her, I let her know she's mine.

And I won't let her go unless she wants it, and with every arch of her back up into me, every time she begs me for more, I know she wants and needs it.

I feel white-hot pleasure rushing up my shaft as my balls tighten along with the rest of my groin, and as it shoots up into her pussy, I let out a deep, rough groan into the room.

The first shot is so satisfying, so strong and fierce, that I can even feel her tumble into her own orgasm with it, and she gasps sweetly as more and more of my seed empties out into her.

After what feels like an eternity of golden stillness between us while our energy unwinds together, I slide out of her, watching my seed drip onto her ass from the tip of my still-stiff cock. Finally, she rolls over to look up at me, and there's a sleepy smile on her face.

"Thanks for the lesson," she says.

I smile and lean in to kiss her deeply, getting one last taste of her before our lips part.

"You still have a lot to learn from me," I say.

Several minutes later, Eva has padded off to the shower to wash herself off. I would have joined her, but as I was putting my pants back on, it occurred to me that in all the excitement of the night, I hadn't gotten a chance to look over the thumb drive yet like I'd planned to.

I don't like putting plans off, so I sit down to start combing through the files while I listen to the soothing sound of shower falling in the background.

There is something soothing about the knowledge that Eva is here. The little signs of her presence, like the shower and the occasional food wrapper left out or her footsteps in the morning, they all made me feel... better about being here, somehow.

Whatever the feeling is, it is all new.

But as I sift through all the useless information on the thumb drive, I can't help but be distracted by a pang of guilt at what I am doing with Eva.

No matter what we say to each other or in our heads in the heat of the moment together, she *is* broken. I practically bought her with the property, and god knows what kind of psychological damage she must have from being down there so long. She has a life to get back to.

And yet, she stays here with me.

She's had plenty of chances to run. It wouldn't be

that hard, I think to myself. I made this place diffi-cult to get into, but easy to get out of. She isn't even locked in. She could slip out at night or while I'm in the shower and make it through the woods to the town and find help. Hell, she could even get me arrested.

But she's still here, getting closer and closer to me by the day.

As those thoughts tug at me, though, something catches my eye on the screen. I sift through a few emails, and my eyes widen.

Just as they do, I hear Eva coming up behind me. Wearing fresh clothes and her hair still dripping wet, she wraps her arms around my neck and plants a kiss on my cheek, to my surprise.

"Well, hello," I say, cracking a smile at her.

"Hey," she says, and I'm struck by how much her face is glowing as she looks at me. I don't have long to dwell on it, though—she peers at the screen and raises an eyebrow.

"What're you looking at?"

"I found something interesting," I say, turning back to the screen. "It's an email between your brother and someone I recognize."

"Someone you recognize?" The worry in her voice tells me she understands how serious that could be.

"Mink wasn't the only man with mafia ties Blake was in touch with," I say, stroking my chin, gesturing to the email on the screen. "This guy he talked to here, they call him 'Jackrabbit' Jamie. He's a slimy little shit, not very professional, but he knows people. Manages to keep his unwashed hands in everyone's dish. This might have been the guy Blake used to find Mink. Could still be an active contact."

"Oh my god…" Eva says, her shining eyes getting wider. "You're not thinking about…?"

"Paying him a visit?" I ask, giving her a judicious look. "I am. This might be our best lead yet. Is that going to be a problem?"

She hesitates, and she opens her mouth to speak.

A soft alarm goes off.

My eyes snap to one of the security feeds I have rigged up to my computer, and it shows me the road leading up to the property.

There's a police car heading up the driveway.

My fist tightens.

"*Fuck.*"

EVA

"*R*un! Hide!" Sal hisses to me, and I take off, bolting out of the room. There's an attic. That's the safest place for me to hide, I think. Just in case that cop decides to barge into the house, the attic is the last place he would look, I assume. I sure as hell can't just stand here gawking in the living room, waiting for him to discover me like a sitting duck.

This is dangerous, not just for me, but for Sal. Between his being on the run from the mafia and the fact that my half-brother thinks I'm already dead, it could be catastrophic if the two of us are discovered here hiding out together. I shudder to think what would happen to us. We have to play it safe.

Besides, the property is under Sal's name, not mine.

Hopefully he can talk the cop out of doing a search, calm him down, relieve his concerns.

God, I hope he can.

I scurry into the converted garage, which is musty and caked with thick dust. I immediately start coughing as I flounder around looking for a light switch. I find it, but flipping the switch achieves nothing. The light's out, and probably has been for ages. With every step, I can feel cobwebs brushing against me as I trudge through the darkness with my hands out in front of me. Finally, my hands touch along something hard and a little dangly. It's the step ladder that leads up to the attic. I hate to think how long it's been just hanging down like this, unfolded and exposed to termites and spiders. I give it a light tug and grimace. It does not feel particularly stable, like it could come crashing down at any moment. But I don't know how else to get up there, and I can hear the wheels of the police car crunching over the messy gravel driveway.

There's no time to worry. I just have to act.

Gritting my teeth and closing my eyes, I grab hold of the step ladder and hoist myself up, scur-rying from rung to rung into the filthy old attic. I open my eyes and blink a few times, struggling to let my eyes adjust to the near pitch darkness. I feel my way around, my hands getting coated in thick dust and grime. I wrinkle my nose and shiver, but I have to keep moving. I know that if I crawl forward far enough, I can find myself in the part of the attic that hangs over the front porch. That way I might have a better chance of eavesdropping on the conversation Sal is going to have with that cop. I need to know what's going on so I can decide my next move.

If the police officer decides to come in and look around with a warrant or something, I might be in big trouble. I need my idiotic brother to keep thinking I'm dead. And if the cop finds me here, not only would Blake find out his murderous plot failed, but the cops might blame Sal for kidnapping me or something.

My heart stumbles at that thought. I don't want to think about that, Sal being in trouble. Well, bigger trouble than he's already in. Especially because it would be my fault. My fault for falling into his lap while all he was trying to do was lie low and hide out. My fault for being too afraid of the cops and the judgment from my employers. My fault for feeling attracted to him, and wanting to lose my virginity to him right away.

Now he's going out on a limb for me, trying to rescue me from my own awful predicament instead of focusing on keeping himself safe. It is noble of him, but it's dangerous as well. And I'll be damned if I end up being the reason he goes down.

Why is the cop here?

For me or for Sal?

Then another idea occurs to me: maybe the cop

is here to investigate Geoffrey Mink. After all, he was the former proprietor of this property, and from what Sal has said about him, Mink surely had plenty of run-ins with the local police for his sexual misconduct and general douchebaggery. In the attic, I keep crawling, trying to force myself to ignore how disgusting this place is. I just took a shower and now I'm covered in probably years' worth of grime.

Gross.

Come on, Eva. Focus. You can always take another shower once you get out of here, but you have to survive this first. Keep your priorities in line, I tell myself harshly.

I freeze up at the sound of a car door slamming shut, followed by the crunch-crunch of heavy foot-steps on gravel. I gulp back my fear and try to stay as still as possible. There's some light filtering through the flimsy wooden floor of the attic where I'm crouched like an animal, and I realize that I can just barely make out the dark moving shape of Sal underneath me on the porch. The footsteps get louder and louder, until they're no longer on gravel. They're walking on wood. Up the steps to the porch. The cop is now standing in front of Sal. I can catch the occasional glimpse of his dark silhouette, and there's a tense silence between the two men.

I cover my mouth with my hand, trying to muffle the sound of my labored breathing. My heart is racing so quickly it feels like I can hardly get enough air into my lungs. But I need to remain quiet so that the cop doesn't catch wind of my location. I need him to think Sal is alone here on the property. My presence would ruin everything, disrupt the very delicate balance of safety and comfort we have here for the time being.

It feels like ages before anyone speaks.

Then, finally, Sal says calmly and coolly, "How are you today, Officer? Can I help you with anything?"

I hold my breath, waiting for the response.

The cop says slowly, "Sir, are you alone on the premises?"

My heart sinks. Oh no. That's not a good start.

But Sal is cool as a cucumber.

"Yes, sir. Just me and my tools."

I almost smile at how quaint and country it sounds. Sal is clearly playing a part here, trying to make himself as innocuous and innocent as possible to the cop.

"Your... your tools?" repeats the officer.

"Yes. I'm sure you've noticed this place is in dire need of a reboot," says Sal. "Just bought the place and it's going to be a lot of work bringing it back to life."

"The property is yours?" asks the cop, sounding a little surprised. But why?

"Yes, sir. Recent purchase of mine and I'm already starting to wonder if I might have made a mistake. Bitten off a little more than I can chew," says Sal.

"What is your name?" asks the cop. My whole body goes cold.

Don't tell him your real name, I think, wishing I could transport these thoughts directly into Sal's head. *Lie. Make something up.*

"My name? Saul Argento," lies Sal matter-of-factly. "Nice to meet you, Officer…?"

"Officer Kennedy," he answers. "Seneca Falls P.D."

I almost heave an audible sigh of relief. Just local police. Not even a Rochester city cop. Suddenly this feels a lot less harrowing. I know it's a messed-up stereotype, but I can't help but feel less threatened by a humble small-town police officer than a street-smart city cop.

Especially in Seneca Falls. Growing up in Rochester, I have obviously been aware of Seneca Falls, though I've never visited. There's not much to visit for. It's just a tiny speck on the map with a few houses and a lot of woods. It actually never even occurred to me that Seneca Falls would have its own police force, but I suppose it makes sense.

"You know anything about the former tenant here?" asks Officer Kennedy.

"Hmm. No. I don't think I do. I bought the property under foreclosure and by the time I arrived, the previous inhabitants were gone," Sal says innocently.

He's doing a bang-up job of acting. Even I'm starting to be convinced.

The officer's demeanor appears to instantly soften, and he takes on a low, conspiratorial tone. "Well, just between you and me, folks around here will be awfully glad to see the former tenant gone," he says, reaching out to nudge Sal's shoulder.

"Oh? Why's that?" Sal asks, leaning forward as though he's interested in the gossip.

"Can't say too much about it. Police business, you know. But I can tell you that old Geoffrey Mink was one sour character. Crotchety old man holed up in this place like a recluse."

"A recluse? Why?" Sal presses on. I'm amazed at how quickly he's turned the tables. Now he's the inquisitor instead of the one being questioned.

"Folks in town damn near drove him out," Kennedy explains. "Mr. Mink was not well-liked in this neck of the woods. Always hanging around playgrounds and schoolyards, wearin' out his welcome. Loitering. Being suspicious. Can't tell you how many times I got called in to question him for trying to chat up an underage girl at a bus stop or something like that. One time a gym teacher caught him trying to sneak into the girls' locker room at the high school. He was just an awful old man. A pervert. Kids up at the school used to call him Mr. Stink. Not a very nice nickname, but he good and well earned it."

"Wow," Sal says, letting out a low whistle. "Sounds like a terrible neighbor."

"You betcha," Kennedy agrees readily. "Glad to see he's moved on. I came out here because I got a call about some strange noises, but I can see now it was probably just the sounds of construction going on. Lots of work to be done here. So, you're gonna try and patch up the place, you said?"

"Yes, sir. It'll be a long project, I'm sure, but I'm up for it."

"Any particular reason why you wanted the property in the first place? Seneca Falls is a nice place, but it's a little off the beaten track. A small town. It's not every day we get someone brand new out here."

"I got tired of city living," Sal lies smoothly. "Just wanted a fresh start somewhere quiet and peaceful. Seneca Falls seems perfect for that."

Yeah, that's right. Butter him up, I think with a grin.

"Oh, you sure did come to the right place then, Mr. Argento," the officer says, puffing out his chest proudly. "Well, if you have any problems or questions, don't hesitate to ask. We're all good neighbors out here. We look out for one another."

"I do appreciate that, Officer. Thank you," Sal says, and I can just picture him wearing that gorgeous, brilliant smile. "Good to meet you."

"Great to meet you, too, neighbor," says the officer, turning to walk away. I start to relax at the sound of his footsteps crunching over gravel. He's heading back to his car, and soon I can wiggle out of this horrible, filthy attic once the coast is clear. But then, suddenly, the footsteps stop. I hold my breath, worried that maybe the cop has caught wind of something worth investigating further. But Sal did such a good job!

"Oh, and before I forget," says the officer in the same jovial voice, "I would be remiss if I didn't mention this. The whole region's got a bulletin out about a missing person. I'm sure it has nothin' to do with Seneca Falls, but just keep an eye out, okay? It's a woman called Eva Wells."

Before I can stop myself, I let out a gasp of shock to hear my own name.

A loud enough gasp that there's no way the cop didn't hear it.

"Whoa," says the officer, taking a few steps closer to the porch. "What was that?"

SALVATORE

$\mathcal{M}$y whole body tenses for a split second as the cop looks up at the ceiling. That noise had come from Eva, no doubt about it to me.

But as smoothly as I've handled the rest of the situation, I let out a groaning sigh, putting my hands on my hips and narrowing my eyes at the ceiling.

"Ah. That'll be the 'roommates' that came with the house. Raccoons hiding out for the winter. I've been meaning to get someone out here to take care of them, but you know how time gets away from you."

Officer Kennedy watches the ceiling for a few moments longer, and my mind races with things I might have to do to get out of the situation. It's been racing with those thoughts ever since I first opened the door.

A smile finally cracks on his face, and he crosses his arms.

"Oh, I hear you. I had one in my shed for the longest time, and my little niece gave him a name before I could call pest control." He shakes his head, laughing. "Had to tell her he'd gone on a trip with his family when I finally got around to it."

"Kids," I say with a laugh.

"Right," the officer says, turning to me with a curt nod. "Well, like I said, keep an eye out. Sorry to bother you, but if you're ever in town and hit the bar, tell the bartender to get you a pitcher on my tab."

"I appreciate it, officer," I say with a chuckle as he heads out the door. "Have a good night."

"And merry Christmas!" he says with a friendly wave, and I wave back to him, watching him get into his car and pull off down the road.

I shut the door just before he's out of sight, then let out a deep breath of relief.

"You're clear," I call up to Eva.

"I am *so* sorry!" she gushes from up above, and when she comes down, I catch her in a tight hug, giving her back a gentle squeeze.

"You're alright," I say, "you did far better than I would have hoped."

"I almost got us found!" she said, half-laughing, half-holding back tears. She sniffed and wiped one away. "Sorry, that was just a little intense."

"It can be a little daunting, hearing your own kidnapping talked about," I say as she steps back, and I give her a reassuring smile. "But you should take a little comfort in that."

"Why?" she says, tilting her head to the side.

"It means you haven't been forgotten," I say, and it takes her a few moments to get the full impact of that, but when it hits, tears come back to her eyes, and she hugs me again—this time just throwing her arms tight around my torso.

"Come on," I say, "that's more than enough excitement for one day."

As I get ready for bed, it hits me how odd the last few hours have been. I'm not used to being protective or giving comfort, but it seems to come to me naturally with Eva, like an instinct I never knew I had.

It's not a bad feeling, either.

I shake it from my mind.

I hear my door creak when I come out of the bathroom from brushing my teeth, and I see Eva standing there in her usual t-shirt and underwear, having grabbed another quick shower to wash off the attic grime. Just the sight of her makes my cock start to swell, and the wide-eyed look she's giving me only tugs at my heartstrings more.

"Hey," I say.

"Hey," she says back. When I raise an eyebrow at her, she continues. "I was just wondering about, well, what happens now. Now that we know what you found out about Blake's 'friend.'"

"I'm going to go see him tomorrow," I say simply. She doesn't need to know more than that, but I can tell by her falling face that it's all she needs to know.

"I was afraid you were going to say that."

"I could tell you about the kind of man he is, if that will help."

"I don't want to think about that before bed," she says with a feeble smile. "Do you... do you mind if I sleep in here tonight?"

I pause, looking at the large bed and thinking for a moment. I shouldn't. I know I shouldn't. And yet…

"Sure," I say with a smile. The way she brightens up at that simple world fills me with warmth. As we get under the covers together and I feel her warm body near mine, I feel more relaxed than usual.

She drifts off to sleep in a matter of minutes, and I lie awake, watching her chest rise and fall with each breath.

There's so much wrong with me keeping her here at my side.

But after all this time... it feels like a mistake we both want to make.

THE NEXT DAY, I watch the clock hit 6:00 PM on my car's dashboard.

It's already dark outside and has been for some time. Most people are home from work already and settling in for a nice evening.

I, on the other hand, am parked outside a run-down apartment, watching a rat scurry across the sidewalk and listening to a dog barking in the distance as I stare up at the apartment window where I know Jerry is.

I did a little research on him to track him to this place. It wasn't hard, for me.

People like Jerry are slippery. There's one good way to deal with that without getting too deep in the muck or risking a knife in your back.

Stepping out of the car, I take a breath and head into the apartment complex.

In what passes for a lobby, there are two sullen-looking teenagers talking quietly to each other. One of them looks like he's about to stop me with a snide look on his face, but I cast him a glare that makes the both of them avert their eyes.

I'm not in the mood to trifle with the small fishes.

As calmly as if I were going to a regular business meeting, I make my way up the stairs, hands in my jacket pockets. Every now and then, I cast a glance over my shoulder to make sure I'm not being followed by someone braver than those kids. This is the kind of place to watch yourself.

Eventually, I make it to the fourth floor, room

406. I make my way up to it, check the gun strapped to my side, and I knock.

I can hear a television on behind the door. There's a pause before I hear someone trying to sneak up to the door quietly. At last, the door handle turns, and it cracks open just enough to peer through the gap. A green eye looks up at me behind the little chain holding the door shut.

Before he can jump away and try to shut the door, my leg flies out and kicks it open.

"Fuck!" Jerry cries as he stumbles back, the door flying in his face and knocking him to the ground at the same time that the door chain gets ripped from the wood and hits the ground uselessly.

Wearing my usual all-black attire, I step into the apartment, light behind me making me look even darker as I move toward Jerry.

The fear in his eyes is so intense that he must think he's hallucinating.

"Oh- oh god, no!" he stammers. He has fallen on his back, giving me a full look of him and everything in his meager apartment.

He's a thin, tall man with a wispy mustache that gives him a rat-like face. The carpet is old and stained, and it smells like mothballs in the room. There's a porno playing on the television, and I see a half-drunk bottle of bourbon on the table in front of the couch.

"Hell of a way to spend Christmas Eve, Jerry," I

say as I push the door shut behind me. It's broken now, so I just slide a nearby chair in front of it to give us some privacy.

"What the hell are you doing here?!" he splutters, looking like he's about to piss himself. I act as casually as if I were here to have a normal conversation, turning around and taking a few steps toward him.

I then pull out my gun and point it at him.

"Dealing with you," I say simply.

"Waitwaitwait! Shit," he stammers, looking around desperately and seeing no weapon, nor anything to help him. "Fuck, how did you get here? Look, Sal, I-I-I don't know what you want!"

"Has that ever mattered?" I say, watching him back up to the back of the couch with his hands up, still on the ground. I can practically see his heart pounding out of his chest. "You know how I operate."

"Fuck," he breathes again. "Look, I don't know who sent you, but—was it the bartender? I didn't mean for all that shit to happen with his sister, I swear to god she said she was eighteen, I-"

"Shut up," I say, moving toward him and raising my gun. Jerry is the kind of man you don't have to dig into far before you start finding the worst of the worst details. I already don't want to turn that stone over.

Besides, I already have a lie to get him to talk.

"You should be proud, Jerry," I say. "You're a loose

end getting tied off by someone with a lot of power. That's quite an accomplishment, for you."

"What?" he sputters, and then recognition comes over his face. "Oh my god, it's that spoiled fucker, isn't it? Blake Brighton?" He runs a hand through his hair, suddenly smiling nervously. "Hey, listen, that guy's an even bigger piece of shit than me, okay? Look, j-just, I'll tell you anything you want to know about him, alright? I can have a ticket to Mexico and a new ID card in two days, and it'll be just like you did the job! He'll never know, the kid's a complete dipshit!"

That was easier than I thought.

Of course, bargaining like that never sways me. I've killed more convincing men than Jerry who've offered me even more. I'm not a man who can be bought off once I'm after my prey. I have a plan for Jerry, though.

"That does make your position interesting, doesn't it?" I say. "But that depends on what you have to say."

"Jesus, everything!" he says, hands shaking as he realizes he might have a little hope. "The kid's a snot-nosed brat with more money than he knows what to do with. What do you want to know?"

"Why does a corporate heir like Blake Brighton want a rat like you dead? Let's start there."

He takes a deep breath, trying to regain his will.

"Probably because I helped the fucker kill that little Cinderella project of a sister."

"What?" I demand, feigning ignorance.

"Kid's the son of Kirk Brighton, that giant-ass office building looming over downtown," he says. "Turns out, his dad has some bastard daughter he ignored for years. When he got sick, Blake took over the business. Guess Blake must have been fucking things up, because when Blake contacted me, he kept going on about his bitch of a sister getting the company instead of him."

I furrow my eyebrows.

"So you helped kill this girl?" I growl.

"No! I mean, I put Blake in touch with Geoffrey Mink, the old guy who used to work for your bosses. Why do you care?"

It takes a lot of willpower not to blow him away right then, if he knowingly subjected any woman to that horrible man. Just a little more time is all I need.

"It's your lucky day, Jerry. Don't play dumb, you've heard what I did in New York. My bosses are dead by my hand, and I need someone with connections to help me stay out of sight. Is Blake not smart enough to realize Kirk will find out about all this?" I ask. "It didn't take much to find you—this is a murder in a shallow grave."

"Won't matter after tonight," he says with a wretched smile.

"Speak English," I demand, taking a step closer, and he puts his hands up further in terror.

"Blake's put a hit out on Kirk! I helped set him up again!" he whimpers, cringing up as much as he can.

"What?" I say, my eyes going wide.

"Old guy's in the hospital, Blake wanted it taken care of tonight, when it would be a skeleton staff watching him!" Jerry says hurriedly. "If you want blackmail on the guy, I-I-I've got his correspondences in the drawer! Let me just-"

POP.

One quick shot from my silenced pistol puts Jerry's brains all over the back of his couch.

The world is a better place without him.

I stride into his bedroom, rummage through the drawers, and rip out the documents I need, barely giving them a glance before I hurry out of the room and make my way back down to the car.

There are hitmen after Eva's father.

What I told Jerry about needing protection might have been true at one point, but as I peel out of the driveway, I realize that I'm doing this for more than just me, now.

I'm doing it for Eva.

But I've got to race against time.

EVA

"Oh my god, oh my god," I murmur to myself as I pace up and down the hallway. I've been at this so long I'm surprised I haven't worn a path into the old wooden floors by now. I glance up at the antique clock ticking away on the wall, my stomach churning with nervousness. I have lost track of how long Sal's been gone, but I know it's been too long. I've been trying to reassure myself that he can handle whatever he encounters out there. I mean, he's a hitman for the mafia. Well, at least he's a former hitman for the mafia. He's got enough kills under his belt to make him way more dangerous than anyone else he runs into. That's got to count for something, right?

Still, I can't stop worrying. I know it's unhealthy, but I can't help but feel incredibly anxious and fearful when he's not nearby. I worry for his safety.

He may have recovered quickly enough from that bullet that swiped his arm and that blow to his face, but he's still so reckless and courageous that it scares me. I know this is probably just run of the mill business for him. A day of reconnaissance and ass-kicking is probably just another day at the office for a tough guy like Sal. But I still can't keep myself from obsessing over all the things that could go wrong.

And apart from worrying about Sal, I also worry about myself.

It's crazy. As soon as he leaves the room, I feel absolutely compelled to follow him, to cling to him like he's a life preserver and I'm floating adrift in the open sea with sharks circling under the surface. When he's gone, I don't even feel like myself. I feel broken and afraid, a shell of who I used to be. I mean, before all this happened with Blake and my father and Geoffrey Mink, I considered myself a pretty independent, tough lady. If there was a spider in my apartment, I took care of it. If some rude guy was harassing me at work, I handled it. If my landlord tried to pull something over on me and charge extra one month, I stopped him in his tracks and told him exactly where he could stick that extra charge. Of course, underneath all that toughness, I have always been vulnerable. Touchy, even. But until now, nobody has managed to get under my skin far enough to reach that part of me. And now that Sal has chipped away at the brick walls around my heart, there's no going back.

I know I'm falling for him.

Whether it's stupid or brash or whatever, I can't stop this train from rolling down the tracks. This is my reality now. Pacing in the hallway of a broken-down safe house, waiting for the man who saved me to return in one piece from whatever risky adventure he's off on out there in the world.

At the click of the front door, I stop pacing and freeze, my eyes going wide with fear. Is that Sal? Or some stranger trying to break in? Maybe it's that nosy Officer Kennedy back to snoop around while Sal's not home.

I crouch down and creep over to the window, parting the blinds just enough to peek out. My shoulders relax when I catch a glimpse of the car in the driveway. Sal's car. Thank god. I hurry to the front door to meet him, grinning ecstatically. Every time he returns to me in one piece, it's cause for celebration in my book. But my smile quickly fades when I see the grim look on his face. I reach up and caress his cheek, my anxiety rushing back.

"Hey, what's wrong? How did it go?" I ask. He sighs.

"It went okay. I'm fine. I handled the situation. But Eva, we have a new problem and I'm not sure how to phrase it to you so I'm just going to say it," he begins, his voice dangerously serious. Sorrowful, even. "The man I interrogated tonight informed me of another deadly plot orchestrated by your bastard half-brother."

"What? What is it? What did Blake do this time?" I demand, wringing my hands. "Is he coming here? Did he somehow find out I'm alive? Oh god."

"No, no. It's got nothing to do with you this time. As far as I can tell, Blake still believes you're dead," he says quickly.

"Then what?" I exclaim.

"It's your father. Did you know he was gravely ill?" Sal asks.

My heart skips a beat. "Yes. Well, no. I knew he was some kind of sick, but I didn't know how bad it was. Is it bad? Oh, it's bad, isn't it?" I ramble, biting my lip.

Sal nods. "Yes. He's in the hospital. Has been for some time, apparently."

"The hospital?" I breathe, scarcely able to comprehend it.

"In a coma," he adds softly. I look up at Sal, horrified.

"That's... that can't be true. He was sick, but he wasn't that bad when I saw him. I know it's been a month, but he can't be in a coma," I say, shaking my head.

"It's true. And that's not the worst of it," Sal says. "I need to prepare myself. Follow me while I explain."

He walks briskly across the house to the bedroom, where he starts stripping out of his clothes and changing into an all-black outfit, then hurriedly packs up a bag with weapons. So many weapons that it makes me wince to see them. As he gets ready— for what, I don't know— he explains. "Blake is impatient. He wants your father dead sooner rather than later."

"What? But Blake... Blake was raised by my father. They're close. He got everything, the picture perfect life, the yachts, the cars. He had *everything* I could never even dream of, growing up," I retort, confused. "Why would Blake want to hurt him?"

"Because he cares more about money than family," Sal says simply. "He can't wait for your father to die so he can swoop in and take all his assets. Besides, in a family like theirs, I imagine Blake spent much more time being raised by nannies than by his own father."

My mood darkens, thinking of Blake taking so much for granted. My mother and I scrounged for everything we ever had, working hard, skipping meals, trying to make something of our lives. We did everything we could, just so I could go on and slowly work on becoming a nurse.

The money my father had would have solved almost all of our problems, but it's more than that. It isn't just the wealth, it's what being a real family could have done. I could have *had* someone when mom passed. I could have grown up with two parents who loved and spoiled me.

Bitterness grips my heart until I realize that I like who I am, and if my father had been in my life, everything would have been different. There's the butterfly effect, but then there's a man being in my life since I was born, the ripples touching every single aspect of my personality, of my world.

And if I like who I am, then I have to accept that I got the better end of the deal.

"So what is going on?" I press him.

Sal stops and looks at me apologetically. "He's planning to have your father killed tonight. At the hospital."

"What?" I burst out, feeling like someone has kicked the air out of my lungs. I fall back to the bed, weak in the knees. "That's ridiculous!" I might not want to change the past, but to kill someone just for their money...

To kill his own father?

"Is it?" Sal says, raising an eyebrow. "Eva, he already hired someone to kill you."

"Yeah, but he doesn't know me. We're strangers. As far as he's concerned, I'm a perfect stranger who's threatening his shot at inheritance," I reason.

"Are you defending him?" Sal says, looking at me sidelong. I frown at him.

"What kind of question is that? Of course I'm not

defending him. I'm just appealing to logic, here," I reply, putting my hands on my hips.

"Look, I'm telling you the truth, but I don't have time to stand here and try to convince you of how evil your brother is," he responds.

"Half-brother," I correct bitterly.

"Either way, he's got a hit out on your father, and considering the fact that he's a fragile old man in a coma, I don't think he has much of a shot at defending himself from the attack," he says. "So I'm going to the hospital. To protect him and stop that hit from happening. But I need to hurry. You stay here and keep your head down."

"What?" I shout. "No! You're not going to the hospital alone."

"Yes, I am," he says firmly. "It's not safe for you. Eva, this isn't Geoffrey Mink we're talking about. This is another man. Perhaps even a team. Willing to murder a comatose old man for money. You cannot come with me. You'll stay here."

"Like hell I will!" I shoot back, throwing up my arms. "Whether or not this hit goes down, my father is lying in a hospital bed. If Blake doesn't kill him first, his illness will probably end his life before too long. I am not going to miss this chance to see him before he dies."

"I thought you had no relationship with him? He's a stranger to you, Eva. It isn't worth risking your life just to see him," Sal lectures me. "Besides, he's in a coma. He wouldn't even know you were there."

"I don't care," I say through gritted teeth. "This could be my last chance to see him. My last chance to say... what needs to be said."

"Even if he can't hear or understand you?" Sal says pointedly.

"Yes."

"Even if it puts your life in serious danger?"

"Yes."

"Even though I am warning you that this is absolutely the worst idea in the world?"

"Hell yes."

Sal groans and pinches the bridge of his nose in frustration. I stare at him defiantly. "I trust your judgment, I really do, but this is my choice, Sal. He's my father. Regardless of what our relationship is like, he's my dad. I need to see him. It's imperative."

He stares at me for a long moment, then sighs. "Fine. You can come along. But you must listen to every word I say and do not disobey me for any reason."

"Got it," I reply.

"Now, let's get going," Sal says. "We've got a murder plot to divert."

* * *

WHEN WE ARRIVE at the hospital, it's nearly midnight.

214

I've been lying in the backseat of the car the whole ride, hiding out in my black clothing. The hospital has Christmas lights twinkling in the trees out front, reminding me that this is Christmas Eve. For all the children of the area, this is prime Santa time. They're all probably lying in bed too excited to sleep, dreaming about the presents they'll find under the tree in the morning.

Meanwhile, Sal and I are stealthily sneaking into a hospital the only way we know how: through the front door. We walk into the hospital, which has only a few lights still on dimly. Being that it's Christmas Eve, there's only a skeleton crew working tonight, and it's eerie to see how empty and lonely the hallways are. Sal moseys up to a nurses' station and sweet talks the elderly nurse into telling him what room my father is in. At first, I think he's crazy. There's no way that could work. But it does. Sal is so charming and handsome he could probably get any information out of anybody anytime. It's impressive and a little bit frightening how convincing he can be. Still, the nurse tells him that it's way past visiting hours, so we'll have to come back in the morning. But that's not the plan.

Once the coast is clear, Sal and I sneak down the hall and take the elevator upstairs, searching for my father's suite. It doesn't take us long to find it, the two of us pressed against the walls, peeking around corners, checking to make sure nobody is watching us. I'm sure somewhere there are video cameras rolling, but I have a feeling the security crew might be a little distracted and sleepy this time of night on Christmas Eve. They're all probably antsy, thinking about how badly they want to go home and be with their families. I know the drill. I've pretty much always been at work over the holidays. It's a lonely gig, working while all your coworkers are home enjoying themselves.

"Just down the hall there," Sal whispers to me, his voice barely audible. The hallways are so quiet you could hear a pin drop, except for the occasional cough or groan from a hospital room or the beep of a machine. So we need to be silent.

I follow Sal down the hall to stand in front of my father's suite. I stand in tiptoes to look through the little square window, and if I crane my neck I can just barely catch a glimpse of his body lying stiffly on a bed, a blue blanket pulled up to his chest. He looks so frail and small, nothing like the authoritative man from our legal meeting. I don't know what illness he has, but whatever it is, it's ruined him. Despite everything, it brings tears to my eyes. We may not be close, but it's still difficult to see one's father this way.

"I need to get in there," I murmur. Sal puts a hand on my shoulder.

"No, Eva. That's a bad idea and you know it."

I turn to look at him, frowning. "Why? Why can't I go see my father?"

"Because he's got a target on his head and I'll be damned if I let you stand in harm's way," he growls. "It's not happening. You've seen him, now go back down to the car while I figure out how to stop this hit from happening."

"No. Hell no. I'm going in there whether I have to pick the lock myself or not."

Sal groans, shaking his head. "You're not going to let this go, are you?"

"No, I'm not. I didn't come here and risk my life just to stare at him through the window. I need to be in that room, Sal," I explain quietly. "The door is locked. How do I get in?"

He holds up a set of master keys and my eyes widen. "Where the hell did you get that?"

He smiles faintly. "I poached it from the nurses' station while that old bird was gawking at me," he explains. I roll my eyes and take the keys from him.

"You're lucky you're so good-looking," I tell him, fiddling with the keys until I find one that fits in the door. It clicks open and I walk into the room. My father's breathing is shallow, ragged. He's hooked up to all kinds of machines. Normally, with my nursing training, I could probably make some sense of them. But this isn't just some random patient. This is my father. My own flesh and blood. All I can do is stare at him and try not to cry.

Sal steps in behind me and locks the door. "Go ahead," he says. "Say what you need to."

Hesitantly, I pull up a stool and sit down by his bedside. This is the first time in my life I've ever gotten a good look at my father. He has the same straight nose I have, but apart from that, he looks nothing like me. It's hard to believe that I'm related to him. This is the man who helped give me life and then turned away from me like I was nothing.

I try to be angry at him, but right now, all I feel is sadness.

"Hey," I begin softly, reaching to take his cold hand. "It's me, Eva. Your daughter. I know this is weird because we hardly know each other, but I had to see you for myself. Here's thing: I want to hate you. In fact, I think when I was growing up, there were times I might have even succeeded in hating you. But honestly? I'm not even that angry. I'm just confused. And sad. I don't know why you never wanted me in your life. I don't know what happened to make you turn away. I'm sure if you were awake right now, you wouldn't care about what I'm saying. But I'm going to say it anyway, and luckily, you can't run away from me this time."

I take a deep breath, looking at his wrinkled, peaceful face.

"My mother was a wonderful person, and I can't even be that angry at you for abandoning me because it just meant I got to have my mom raise me.

She made me the strong, tough, smart, independent woman I am today. I know I'm the kind of lady she'd be proud of, but I don't know what you want for me. And it shouldn't matter. You made it clear all those years ago that I don't matter much to you. But still. You're my father. I have spent way too long being angry and hurt and letting that pain make me bitter. Because of you, I have never really let anyone in. Never let anyone get close enough to know the real me. But you know what? I'm done with that. I'm finally learning what it feels like to be vulnerable, and it's scary sometimes, but I think it's good for me. I'm undoing all the pain you left me with. And that will probably make me a better person in the end," I say.

I take another deep breath and continue. "Dad, I'm working really hard to forgive you. I want to. Not necessarily for your sake, but for mine. And if you ever wake up from this, I hope you'll finally see me for who I am, for how well I have survived even without you in my life. But if you don't wake up... just know that I may not forgive you right now, but I'm working on it. I don't want to carry this anger forever. Please wake up. We've got a lot of lost time to make up for, you and me. I don't know if you want that, but I think I do. I think we could try."

A tear rolls down my cheek and drops onto his hand. He doesn't move. I sigh and look back, expecting to see Sal behind me. But he isn't there.

I've been so caught up in talking to my father that I somehow misplaced Sal. My heart starts to race. I don't know where he went or why, but now that I'm alone with my father, it's hitting me just dangerous this is. If my father is the target, then I'm standing directly in the crossfire.

SALVATORE

$\mathcal{I}$ move through the shadows of the half-lit hospital, lights dimmed in the late hours of the night to let the patients rest. My footsteps are silent. I pull on the pair of black leather gloves from my pockets.

Now is the time to hunt.

It's Christmas Eve, and many of the non-essential staff are at home rather than working or visiting in the dark halls of the hospital.

But there are other hunters about, and I have to make them my prey.

We've come at a time that would be good for them to strike—if I were the one carrying out this job, it's when I would come, and I never assume that my enemies aren't as smart as me. That's what's made me so successful over the years. I never underestimate my foes.

I step behind a corner as I hear footsteps approaching, and I watch a group of three nurses discussing some charts pass by. They head down the hall without having seen me.

They're likely nearby, moving with the crowds, but not too closely.

I stay out of sight or look inconspicuous as possible as I watch a few other groups move by. A doctor who looks haggard on his way to change out of scrubs. A small family leaving one of the rooms with emotional looks on their faces. More nurses.

But as an older couple passes by, I spot two figures behind them who catch my eye.

They're dressed like patient care techs, the people who transport and clean patients. Each wears scrubs, but they don't fit very well—one of the outfits is clearly too small for one of the men, and they aren't walking like people who know their way around very well.

I'm not sure yet, though. Once they're a ways ahead of me, I start tailing them, keeping a slow pace and pretending to be distracted by my phone. Every now and then, I glance up at them as they walk.

They're heading in a circle, doubling back around to the ward where Kirk and Eva are. They must be waiting for the foot traffic in the hallway to die down.

When they get to one of the large doors that's

operated only by the barcode scanners on their badges, I get the confirmation I need.

They speed up nearly to a jog to catch up with a nurse and follow her through the doors. They don't have security badges.

As soon as they're through the doors, I jog to catch up with them, and as soon as I slip through the doors, one of them turns his head toward me.

We lock eyes, they look at each other, and they take off in opposite directions.

Fuck.

One of them is heading directly toward where Kirk is, and he's the one I go after first.

He darts down a hallway that's all but abandoned. I don't know how long it will be that way, so I burst into a full sprint after him. He's quick, but I'm quicker.

When I catch up to him, he must have heard me, because he spins around and tries to throw a punch at me wildly. As I dodge it, I notice the gun he has strapped to his torso. I have to act very, very fast.

With a quick jab, I hit him in the nose, making him grunt, and he tries to tackle me, but I sidestep him. He hasn't gone for his weapon yet, knowing what kind of panic drawing a gun in a hospital will cause, but a desperate man will do anything.

Instead of trying to fight me further, though he takes off running again.

Within a matter of seconds, I catch up to him and

grab him around the neck with my arms, wrapping him in a sleeper hold. He struggles fiercely, but the hold I have on him is tight as iron.

Before he has even stopped moving as he slips out of consciousness, I look around at the rooms nearby. I see a sign for a bathroom, and I make my way toward it as the hitman goes limp in my arms.

I drag him inside and prop him up on one of the stalls, locking the door behind us. When I'm sure that he's out cold, I take his head in my bare hands and snap his neck with one hard, swift motion.

Every second counts, and I don't have time to deal with him otherwise. Besides, I can't have killers waking up after we've left.

With the first man dead, I slide out from under the stall and rush out the door to find the second man.

I reason that he has probably looped around toward Kirk's room. I have to head him off. I make my way down the winding hallways back to where I started my hunt.

Surely enough, as soon as I step out onto the hallway, I see the second man halfway down the opposite side.

We lock eyes once again, and he bolts, running carelessly in the opposite direction. He collides with a doctor, sending her and the papers she was carrying flying. Before the doctor even realizes what's happening, I rush past her after the second hitman.

This one is faster than the last, and it's a struggle to keep up with him. He knows as well as me that if we get seen by too many people, we'll be caught, or the police will get involved, so he darts off to the right and heads down a set of stairs.

I follow him, bounding down several stairs at once to keep up with him. Three floors down, he darts out one of the doors, and it's several seconds before I can follow him out.

As soon as I step out onto the floor, I have to hold myself back—this floor is packed with people moving around.

Carolers, if I were to guess based on how they're dressed.

I curse and move through them carefully, my eyes scanning the crowd to find the man again. I can't lose him, not now.

The sound of electric doors moving brings my attention to the elevator, and I turn in time to see the doors of one closing.

The hitman is watching me from inside, standing calmly next to a couple of other nurses with a triumphant look in his eyes.

I clench my jaw. There's no time to wait for an elevator. I dart back into the stair shaft and bound up the stairs as fast as my legs can carry me.

When I make it back to the top of the stairs, I

hurry toward the hallway, rounding the corner in a matter of seconds. My mind races with what could happen if he gets to Eva and Kirk before I do. Eva is tougher than she looks, but this man is armed and dangerous, and he already knows that this isn't going to be a quick and clean job. He's liable to do anything.

When I round the corner, I see him.

His back is facing me, and he's heading for the door to Kirk's room.

I wonder at first why he's not running, but then I see the reason from the opposite side of the hallway. Another nurse is approaching, her head down and eyes focused on a chart in her hands.

I don't have time to lose. I move as silently as I can up behind the hitman, feet not making a sound as I close the distance between us.

My legs carry me closer with every step.

I'll reach him.

The only question is whether I can do anything about it once I'm there, once that nurse is close enough to see us.

*T*he hospital room door clicks open and my blood runs cold.

I jump up and turn around with a gasp, expecting to see some masked man with a knife or something. And in a way, I do see a man like that. But he's a familiar face.

"Sal," I breathe, relief washing over me. "You're back."

"Yes," he says simply, reaching out his hand to me. "I'm here now. Everything is fine."

"Did you...?" I trail off, biting my lip.

He nods as I take his hand. "It's taken care of. The threat has been eliminated. No one will come in and hurt your father. His illness is his only concern now."

I glance back at my dad, lying motionless and

calm on the hospital cot. His eyes are shut, his lips slightly parted as he breathes slow, rattling breaths. If not for those breaths I might think he's dead at first glance. I can't help but wonder how long he has left. It seems unlikely that he will ever recover from this. Tears spring to my eyes again and I quickly swipe them away. Sal comes to stand beside me and put an arm around my shoulders.

"It's okay," he whispers, kissing the side of my head.

"Is it?" I ask tearfully.

"It will be. I promise. But Eva, the longer you're out in public, the more dangerous it is for both of us. We need to get you home," he says.

"Home," I repeat. It feels like I hardly know what that word means anymore. Home doesn't seem to be a physical location. If anything, Sal is my home. He's my comfort, my solace, my safe haven. Anywhere I am with him is home. I have nowhere else to go.

"Yes. Come on," he nudges me. Finally, I give in and start to walk away.

I glance back over my shoulder at the sleeping man on the bed, the near-stranger who gave me life and then dismissed me for twenty-three years. I don't know exactly how I ought to feel about any of this. "Bye, Dad," I murmur as we step out into the dimly-lit hallway. Sal guides me down the hall to the emergency stairs, presumably because everyone else would be taking the elevator. As he opens the door to the staircase, my eyes are drawn to a heaping cart of scrubs. It's such a massive pile that it actually confuses my eye. The shape is strange. Bulky. Shaped almost like… a person.

A body.

My heart starts to race as I realize there's a body in that cart. Probably put there by Sal.

"Come along," he says softly, jolting me back to reality. He might be a dangerous man, but he's a dangerous man who seems to be willing to stop at nothing to protect me and my father. I can hardly fault him for that. If not for him, the two of us might not have survived this night. So I tear my eyes away from the body in the scrubs cart and follow Sal down the many flights of stairs to the first floor.

We wait until the coast is clear, and then we quietly pad down the hall to the exit. Once we're out, we break into a run, darting to his car and getting in before anyone can see us leave. I'm sure we're on the hospital video surveillance system, but at least this gives us a head start. Sal drives us home quickly, but not so quickly as to attract the attention of traffic cops. It's a fairly long drive, the highway getting darker and less maintained as we move farther away from the city and into the woodsy upstate New York countryside. It's still pitch-dark outside, but I know in a couple hours the sun will begin its slow ascent into the sky, casting pale light over the landscape. It strikes me suddenly that this is Christmas Day, technically.

"Merry Christmas," I say suddenly, breaking the silence.

Sal looks over at me, surprised. Then he smiles and reaches across the console to take my hand and squeeze it gently. "Merry Christmas, Eva."

By the time we arrive back at the safehouse, I'm overcome with relief. This place, although it holds the awful memories of being trapped underground, has become a comfort to me. Besides, it was really only the shed and bunker that terrified me. The safehouse itself hasn't done anything against me. In fact, with all the little fixes and improvements that Sal has been doing around the place, it's starting to almost look like a livable residence again. The car rolls to a stop and we get out, trudging up the gravel to the front porch.

As soon as we get in, I go to the kitchen and make us some hot chocolate with a little splash of liqueur added in. Then we sit in the living room, sipping our hot drinks and trying to wind down from this eventful night. I stare down into the gently swirling contents of my mug, my mind running in circles.

"What are you thinking about?" Sal asks gently. I bite my lip, trying not to cry.

"Just about how fucked up my life is," I begin, shrugging. "I never asked for any of this, you know? I just wanted to live my normal, quiet, hard life. It was never fun or exciting but I was finally kind of stable. I had two jobs, my own place, and I was *this* close to finally adopting a cat. Man, I really wanted that cat."

"You do seem like a cat person," he says, smiling faintly.

"I am. And I was looking forward to having some little friend to keep me company when I was off work. It got lonely sometimes, of course. Living the way I did," I admit.

"I can understand that," he says.

"I bet you do. I can't imagine being a mafia hitman is a very social job."

"No. Not at all. It's the perfect job for a loner. A lone wolf."

"That's you, isn't it?" I say, taking a sip of my hot chocolate.

"I was that man once. Now, I'm not so sure," he confesses, looking at me pointedly. My heart does a little flip-flop. I decide to change the subject.

"It's not fair, you know. I never cared much about my father. Sure, it hurt like hell to know that he didn't care about me, but I had my mother. She was parent enough for the both of them on her own. But now that my father is dying... well, suddenly I don't hate him. I hardly even dislike him. I want him to survive, Sal. So that we can get to know each other. I told him I wasn't quite ready to forgive him, and I'm not, but I want to. As soon as I can. I just need him to wake up and get better so I can tell him myself," I ramble.

"I hope he will," Sal says.

"And then there's stupid Blake. My idiot half-brother who despises me. Hates me so much he wants me dead. He doesn't even know me, Sal! He's never had a conversation with me. Sure, we have nothing in common besides a shared father. We were never going to be close friends. But this? This is absurd. It was bad enough growing up without a father, knowing that he abandoned my mom and I and never looked back. But knowing that I have a brother who hates me so much he didn't even hesitate to hire someone to kill me is too much. I know so many people with close, supportive, loving families, and I get stuck with this."

"You're right. It isn't fair," Sal agrees, scooting closer and putting an arm around me. I lean into his touch, his warmth.

"I've always kept to myself. I've been so afraid to rely on anyone, depend on them. Because of how badly my father hurt me when he disappeared without a trace. I've missed out on so much. Close friendships. True love. Instead it's always just been my mother and me, and when she died, it was just me alone. That's all I've ever known, Sal."

"I know what that's like," he says softly. "To isolate yourself. To be alone."

I rest my head on his shoulder. "I just keep wondering what I did to deserve this. I must have really screwed up in a past life or something."

"No, you can't blame yourself for this, Eva. You don't deserve this pain," he says firmly.

"Thank you for saying that, I don't know if I can quite believe it, but thank you," I admit. A tear rolls down my cheek and Sal catches it with his finger. He tilts my head up to kiss me.

"Eva, I have not known you long. But I'm a damn good judge of character. I have to be, for the work I carry out. And I can tell that you are a truly good person. A little broken, perhaps, but so are all the most wonderful people. And so am I," he whispers.

Suddenly, I don't want words anymore. I need more than that. I need comfort, physical comfort. And I know Sal can give it to me. Without a word, I get up and push him back on the couch, straddling his lap. He slides his hands down my body to cup my breasts, my ass. He falls into step with me easily, without saying anything at all. He just knows.

I strip off my shirt and he reaches around to unclasp my bra, tossing it across the room. I lean forward and kiss him deeply while his fingers tweak and roll my nipples, sending streaks of pleasure down through my core. I moan into his mouth, rolling my hips, grinding against his already rock-hard shaft. I can feel it straining under the fabric of his pants, and suddenly I can't wait any longer.

I get up and crouch down in front of him, taking off his shoes, then pulling down his pants and moving them away. He's not wearing boxers. His cock springs free and I lick my lips, wrapping both hands around his enormous length while I look up at Sal expectantly. He gives me a nod and I eagerly pull his massive cock into my mouth, enjoying the sensation of my cheeks aching and stretching to accommodate him. Sal groans and places a huge hand on the back of my head, pushing me down on his cock until I'm nearly choking. I bob up and down, letting his shaft brush against the back of my throat, my tongue swirling around the head of his cock while my hands work his length. I can feel myself getting wetter by the second, turned on by what my mouth and hands can do to Sal. I get a thrill out of making him moan, making him feel so good.

This is exactly the kind of distraction I need. This is the Christmas present I want.

Just as I can feel Sal's balls tightening up, his body tensing in anticipation of climax, he gently nudges me away and beckons for me to stand up. I obey, watching him with hopeful eyes.

"Strip," he says simply.

I take off my shoes, pants, and panties so that I'm

standing fully naked and exposed in front of him. There's a coolness in the house from the gentle snowfall outside, and goosebumps prickle up on my skin.

"Come here," he growls. "I want you to ride my cock."

I dutifully straddle him on the couch, slowly lowering myself down, spearing myself on his massive, hard cock. With every inch, I feel an over-powering shiver of pleasure, moaning as I slide his full length inside me. Sal grabs my hips and starts to rock me, the two of us grinding together passion-ately as his cock strikes my g-spot over and over again. He reaches down between us to rub my clit with his fingers while we fuck, making me cry out. It's not long before my body is seizing up, coming all over his cock.

"Yes. Good girl," he says quietly, darkly. I can tell he loves being in control, being able to make my body do what he wants. I love it, too. I love obeying his every instruction, relinquishing control for once. Being able to actually *trust* someone again. And not just because he saved me. Because he's shown me, with every action, that I can trust him.

If I'd run away to the cops, I could have gotten him put in jail forever, but he trusts me to stay here with him. He didn't threaten me, didn't keep me locked in that bunker. From our very first moment together, he made himself vulnerable for me. He was the man I needed.

And then, when things spiraled out of control and we realized there was a hit out for me, he made himself hard. He went out of his 'retirement' for me. He's killed the worst type of men in the world, and that strength, that power...

It turns me on.

He kisses me as I ride his cock, his hands caressing my full breasts, his fingers circling my nipples and sending spirals of bliss down my body. He kisses my neck, just below my ear, where I'm ticklish in the most delicious way. I shudder and lean into him, delighting in the sensation of pleasure bordering on discomfort. It's wonderful and so, so good.

Suddenly, Sal grabs my hips.

"I'm going to pump you full of my come, sweetheart," he promises in a low whisper. A thrill of excitement rocks my body.

"Yes. Oh god, please," I murmur as he picks up the pace. I know it's risky, and that just turns me on even more. I've been surrounded by so much death. My mother died far too young, and my father is now at death's door. And I was locked in a bunker, facing down death or something worse every minute of the day.

I don't want to think about death anymore.

I just want to think about life. A new life.

I'm on top, but he's in control, bouncing me up and down on his cock while I moan and roll my eyes back. All I can do is hold onto the back of the couch, riding him faster and faster while I come again and again. My sweet honey gushes over his cock, making us both slippery and sticky.

"Oh my god," I whimper. "Oh my god, Sal."

"Oh, fuck. Baby, your pussy is so wet for me," he groans through gritted teeth. "God, you feel like heaven. I want to fuck you forever."

His hips snap erratically as he starts to lose control. He fucks me harder and harder until finally he pulls me close and kisses me, groaning into my mouth as he fills me up with his sweet come. I roll my hips a few times, milking every last drop of his precious seed while we pant and sigh in the after-glow. Sal kisses me softly as a tear rolls down my face. I don't know why I'm crying. I'm not upset. I'm just overwhelmed. He's so intense. Everything has been so intense.

Finally, he moves me off of him and stands up, heading to the shower.

"Where are you going?" I ask, pouting.

"This has to end," he says. My heart skips a beat. What does he mean? What has to end? Us? The two of us together? What we've been doing— what we just did?

He seems to catch on that his words have sent me into a tizzy, because he turns and looks back at me, adding, "The danger. The fear. I can't allow this to keep going any longer, Eva. It's not fair to you. You should not have to hide out here like a criminal. It's not your fault and you deserve better. Your bastard brother has to pay."

My eyes go wide as I get up to follow Sal to the shower. I can feel his seed leaking down my thighs. He turns on the water and we step inside. I grab the soap and start lathering up.

"What are you going to do?" I ask meekly, afraid of the answer.

Sal says firmly, "I'm going to confront him. End this once and for all."

"Sal, he's dangerous."

"So am I," he says, and I know he's right. "Anything he can bring to the table will pale in comparison to me."

"Okay. Well, then, I'm coming with you," I declare. Sal shakes his head.

"No. Not this time, Eva."

"Yes, this time. *Especially* this time," I retort defiantly. "First of all, whatever happens, you'll need a witness on your side. Second of all, he's my brother. I should be there. I-I want to hear him say it. I want to hear his confession, straight from his own mouth." Adrenaline courses through my veins at the thought of it. Sal pulls me into his arms and kisses the top of my head.

"It's not safe for you."

"I don't care," I reply. "Sal, I need to do this."

He looks at me, hard. Sizing me up. I can tell there is not a single cell in his body that wants to allow this. He wants to tell me no. But I stand my ground.

"Sal, let me go with you."

SALVATORE

*H*eavy fog hangs in the air as I walk through the empty graveyard, no sound around me the hooting of an owl in a distant tree. My footsteps don't even make noise.

One of the things I was able to grab from Jerry's apartment was his contact information, which in turn gave me access to his accounts.

So, I impersonated him, and I set up a meeting with Blake.

I told him there had been a complication at the hospital, and that we needed to meet up immediately. And so here, in the middle of the night in a graveyard on the outskirts of town, I'm heading to a meeting with Blake Brighton, who expects me to be Jerry, who he no doubt was planning to chew out or even kill, if I know anything about Blake's personality by now.

This isn't just any graveyard, either. This is where the Brighton family has their own private mausoleum.

It isn't an unusual kind of place to meet people in my line of work. Back when I was younger and had a different idea of what dramatic flare was, it was almost like a calling card for me.

Of course, Blake doesn't know that.

As I walk among the dead, I feel their stillness all around me like anticipation being tightly wound up. The moisture of the fog makes the tombstones damp and the ground wet.

The Brighton mausoleum stands like a lonely monument in the fog, a big and dark shadow among shadows. I arrived later than I said to meet him, just to make sure I didn't beat him here.

I want the satisfaction of an entrance.

As I expect, though, Blake didn't come alone. Outside the mausoleum, I see two men standing by the door. One has his arms crossed and leans back against the wall while the other smokes, looking out into the fog. I can see guns at their sides and know they're there for security. My guess would be that he planned to have Jerry dragged before him when he arrived.

I crouch down as I approach. The fog and the gravestones give me cover, and whenever one of them looks my way, I freeze, looking like nothing but a dark shadow out in the sea of stone.

I circle around the back of the mausoleum and slip up the side of it, hugging the wall. The men aren't speaking to each other. I can hear the smoker occasionally inhale on his cigarette.

With no sound and no hesitation, I come around the side of the building and deliver a quick, sharp strike to the neck of the man leaning against the wall. I watch his throat crumple in on itself before I move to the smoker. He barely has time to turn around before I seize him around the throat with my arms in a sleeper hold, and he kicks in silence before finally going limp in my arms.

Both men dealt with, I turn my eyes to the entrance to the mausoleum.

I move into the mausoleum through the stone doorway, and I draw my weapon. I'm here to get answers, but I need to be ready. Someone like Blake isn't likely to be smart about how to handle the likes of me.

Once I'm halfway into the short hallway to the center of the building, I let my footsteps echo, and I hear someone breathe in sharply from the corridor to the left. The inside of the mausoleum is in the simple shape of a cross, with the entrance and three short hallways.

"Is he here?" I hear a man's voice ask in a snide, demanding tone.

"Yes," I say simply as I appear in the corridor as a

tall, dark figure looming at the end of the passage at the intersection.

Blake is a short man, shorter than I expected. His face goes white at the sight of me, but it's already deathly pale, and his blonde hair makes him look almost ghostly. He looks like a childish, softer version of his father, dressed in warm winter clothes from some top-line designer brands in NYC. He looks more like he's about to go out on a yacht than meet a mafia contact in a graveyard.

"Who the fuck are you?" he says, cautiously stepping toward me, looking like he could bolt at any second. "And where the hell are my men?"

"I'm the one they call the Angel of Death," I say, my voice a low, dark tone, each syllable rolling off my tongue with practiced ease. "If you knew anything about dealing with murder, you'd know my name."

He looks chilled to the bone, and his hand twitches as if reaching for something at his side. He hasn't seen my gun yet, but if I planned to just kill him quickly and quietly, he'd have never seen me coming.

"Where's the ratty guy?" he asks, his voice thin. "What the fuck is this?"

"He won't be coming, Blake Brighton," I say. "Nobody will."

Like snow melting away suddenly, Blake loses his will, and his skinny legs break into a run. He darts past me, fumbling with a gun at his side and clumsily shooting back, the bullet hitting stone and chipping some of it off as it ricochets behind me.

Blake takes off out of the mausoleum, and I jog after him.

I'm in no hurry, though. I want to let him tire himself out.

Outside in the cold, wet air, I can see his figure vanishing into the fog, but the sound of his running footsteps makes it easy to follow him, letting him stay just out of reach to give him the slightest glimmer of hope.

"Tell me about your sister, Blake," I call after him as he runs. "Tell me about what you put her through."

"I'm not telling you anything!" I hear his voice call back at me, and I weave through the tombstones as he runs.

He's headed for the exit, so I pick up the pace and circle around him, blocking off his escape and listening to the sound of his footsteps running toward me.

"Do you know how she died?" I ask, moments before Blake's sprinting form appears in front of me. He skids to a halt, and I can see the whites of his wide, terrified eyes. He raises his gun, but by the time he fires, I've already dived out of the way. He takes off running in the opposite direction, deeper into the cemetery.

"You handed her over to the devil himself," I call after him, giving chase.

"Fuck off! I'll have you killed!"

"Your hitman was a monster, Blake," I say. "You condemned an innocent woman to a living hell."

"Who sent you?" he yells, his voice getting hoarse. He's veered off to the right. There are no exits this direction. I crack a smile. I'd forgotten the simple joy of hunting down someone who deserves it. "I'll pay you triple!"

"Money won't save you now, Blake," I say. My tone is plain, matter-of-fact. I'm less of a person, more of a force of nature weighing down on my prey with each passing second. "How long did you think you could hide behind it?"

"Anything you want!" he blurts, his voice sounding panicked. I nearly catch up to him, and he fires blindly at me again. I feel nor show any fear. "My girlfriend's a model, you want her? I can get you anything!"

"Are they even people to you, Blake?" I ask, hearing him starting to pant as he runs out of breath. "Your sister? Your father?"

"Is that what this is about? Did that bastard send you?"

"You're the only one I'm here for, Blake," I say, a hint of deadly pleasure in my tone.

He's clearly running out of places to run. I hear another gunshot go off, and I can only imagine he fired blindly into the dark. I decide it's time to close in on him. I get low and start moving quietly and swiftly, as if I were chasing prey that were really worth my efforts.

All this for Eva, and only Eva.

Because if it were me, I would just end him swiftly and silently.

It isn't long before I get sight of him again, and I let him see me as I rush toward him. He's not an athlete, and he's already sweating and white-faced. He turns and runs full-tilt away from me.

As he does, he comes to a small hill, and in the slick mud of the late night's fog, he slips.

I watch him tumble down the hill after a few frantic tries at getting his balance back. I hear a howl of pain as he twists his ankle on the way down, and he rolls through mud and dew before coming to a stop under a statue of the Virgin Mary.

I stand over the hill, glowering down at him as he pushes himself up and glares back at me. His gun isn't far from him, but he can see mine as plain as day. If he has any sense left in him, he won't reach for his.

After what I've seen of him, though, I won't put it past him.

"What the fuck is this about?" he snarls up at me.

"I know everything about you, Blake Brighton," I say, taking a few slow steps toward him. "But I want a confession from you. I want to hear what makes your heart so cold that you killed your own sister, a woman who'd done nothing in your life."

"Nothing but get in the way!" he shouted, but his voice cracked into a thin squeak. "Is that what you want to hear, you fucking psychopath? I'm the one who grew up with Father, I'm the one who deserves this!"

"Your father wants to give her everything," I say, taking another step. "Why do you think that is?"

"I don't fucking care what that senile old ass is thinking," he spits.

"He probably thinks that you're a *monster!*"

Those weren't my words.

Both Blake and I look right, along the base of the hill.

Eva steps out from behind one of the tombstones, a gun in her hand aimed at Blake.

"*What the fuck?!*" Blake gasps, trying to push himself further away but only backing into the statue. "You—you're supposed to be dead!"

"He locked me away, Blake!" she shouts, holding her gun tight, a furious look in her eyes. "Your hitman just... just took me! I had a *life*, and you just took it away from me for... for just *being* there!"

His face twists into a sneer, like a bratty child's. "That's the whole problem! Father saw *you* and decided he liked you more, for no reason! But you can't prove anything, anyway."

I pull out a copy of the thumb drive full of the

evidence I've collected and photographed over the past few days and hold it up with a smile.

"If we didn't have evidence, we wouldn't be having this conversation. You should have invested in better security at the offices."

His face turns red.

"This is exactly what I mean. I could tell from the moment I saw you that you were always going to be this *bitch* who got in the way of everything I've had going for so long! You and Father have no idea how to make it in the real world. I'm the one who made the connections I had to, and I'm the one who called the hard shots."

"People like you are the great evils in the world," I say in a dark tone. "You're no better than that hitman of yours, preying on vulnerable people because you have the power and can make a quick buck from it."

"You want to be the bigger man, Blake?" Eva says, scrunching her face up and holding back so, so much anger. "Come in with us. I'm going to take you to court for everything you did. For what you did to me, what you tried to do to our father, for every other person you've screwed over."

Blake is breathing heavily, glaring daggers at Eva. For a moment, I could swear I see his face softening. He clenches his fist and relaxes it again, then looks to the ground before him.

In the blink of an eye, he jumps for his gun.

Eva stands back and aims at him as he picks it up and swings the barrel toward her.

There's a gunshot.

The next instant, blood is splattered across the Virgin Mary's plinth as Blake slumps to the ground, a hole from my bullet in his head.

I lower my gun and look over to Eva, who stares at the scene with wide, shocked eyes.

Immediately, I make my way over to her and take her in my arms as she lets hers fall to her sides, stunned at everything.

"He's…"

"He was going to shoot you, Eva," I say, and Eva hugs me, but I don't feel the shudder of sobbing in my arms like I expected. I look at her face, and there are tears there, but she hardens her face and nods, looking at Blake's body again.

"No, you're right," she says, her voice soft but firm. She's got far, far more mettle under the surface that's only just starting to come out. "If anyone caught up in all this deserved it… it was him."

I smile down at her, and she looks up at me with shining eyes that soon give way to a smile of her own. She sniffs and wipes a tear from her eye.

"Is it… does this mean it's over?"

"He's gone, Eva," I say, squeezing her softly, "he can't hurt anyone again. He was at the head of all this. We have so much evidence against him at this point that there will be no question that we acted in self-defense." I brush a lock of hair out of her face. "Don't trouble yourself with that, though. Not yet."

She nods, fighting to hold back tears as she hugs me one more time. Even in the darkness and gloom of the graveyard, with her right there by me... I feel at peace.

The next moment, it shatters.

A buzzing comes from Blake's body.

We both look over and see a cell phone half-hanging out of Blake's pocket, lighting up as it receives a call. We exchange a glance before I walk over to it and pick it up.

"It's the hospital," I say, and Eva looks over to me with a concerned look on her face. I hesitate, then answer the phone.

"Hello?"

"Hello, Mr. Brighton? We need you to come down to the hospital immediately to see your father."

My face goes ashen, and I look to Eva, and I watch just as much dread wash over her as well.

I close the phone.

"We have to go to the hospital. Now."

EVA

"We've got to hurry!" I exclaim, reaching to grab Sal's hand and pull him away from the scene. "Come on! My dad might be in trouble!"

"I'm coming," Sal says quietly, "We'll get there as fast as we can."

The two of us break into a run, leaping over headstones and slipping on the icy, dewy grass in between the graves. My heart is pounding and I can hardly keep one thought straight in my head at a time, I'm so overwhelmed with emotion. On the one hand, I'm conflicted about watching my half-brother die in front of me. Should I feel sad about that? Or just relieved?

It's over, right? I don't have to hide anymore. Sal is a professional. He can find a way to figure out what to do in the wake of Blake's demise. There has to be some kind of mafia protocol for covering up a murder like this. But then that reminds me that Sal is on the run, too. And killing Blake surely will put him back in the spotlight somehow. What if the mafia finds him hiding with me? Where do we go? What do we do?

And at the moment, there is an even more pressing concern: what's happened to my father? I know the hospital would not be calling Blake in the middle of the night like this unless it was an emergency. To be honest, it fills me with rage to know that Blake is my dad's emergency contact, considering that his own son tried to have him killed while he lay helpless in a coma. I can't blame my father for that, really, though. I get the sense that he doesn't have many close allies in his life. Blake was probably the extent of his affection, and even that seems to be somewhat strained.

Strained enough that Dad might try and push me to the center focus of the will and shove Blake aside. I suppose Blake must have royally screwed up handling the manufacturing business to deserve that. And people like Kirk Brighton are all about the money. Blake probably nearly ran the business into the ground or something. I never got the sense that he was particularly responsible.

I shouldn't think ill of the dead, I tell myself. Sure, Blake was a rude, spoiled, narcissistic, mildly sociopathic asshole who paid for someone to try and kill his own sister and father. But still, it seems morally fucked up to think so badly of him after watching him crumple to the ground in front of me. Some small part of my heart aches for the loss, but it's overshadowed by the relief that washed over me the moment I realized he would no longer be able to hurt me or my father. Sal did what he had to do. He always promised he would protect me no matter what it cost him, and he held up his promise.

We finally make it back to the car. Sal throws it into gear and we rumble off down the road, leaving the misty, cold graveyard far behind us as we motor along to the hospital. Sal reaches over to take my hand. I'm trembling all over, and not just from the biting cold.

"Are you alright?" he asks kindly. I shrug.

"I-I don't know yet. I think I'll just have to see what's going on with my father before I can tell you one way or another," I admit.

"I'm sorry about your brother," Sal says, glancing over at me with genuinely sad eyes. I give his hand a squeeze and lift it to my lips to kiss it. I force myself to not cry.

"It's not your fault," I murmur.

"It is. I shot him, Eva. For that I am so sorry," he says firmly.

"You did what you had to. You protected me, Sal. You saved my life yet again. He might have been my brother—half-brother—but it's not like he was ever my family, really. We didn't know each other. And besides, I think he kind of burned that bridge when he hired Geoffrey Mink to do away with me," I explain. "Blake was an awful man and it makes my skin crawl to think that we might have been cut from the same cloth."

"You weren't. Blood does not necessarily make a family. Hell, some of my associates within the mafia were much closer to me than any of my real family. I was never close to anyone related to me. We were family by happenstance. Love makes a family. Loyalty makes a family. Blake showed you neither love nor loyalty, so you should not take his passing so hard. Of course, I can't tell you how to react to such an event. It's not my place to say," Sal remarks.

"I'm just so conflicted. I know I should be sad, and I suppose maybe a very small part of me is sad to see him die this way. But overall? I'm relieved. I hate that I feel this way, but I do. I'm glad he can no longer threaten me or you or my dad," I confess, feeling guilty about celebrating Blake's death.

I wince, thinking about my father. "And my dad... I don't know what is going to happen. I'm so scared, Sal. I know he and I don't have a relationship. Certainly not a father-daughter relationship. I've spent my whole life kind of hating him, actually. But seeing him so helpless and fragile in that hospital bed just shook me to my core. I've already lost my mother, who was the shining light in my life.

I've been so alone until you found me. And now I'm about to lose my father, too. I just don't know how to feel. I was just starting to think I could maybe forgive him and maybe we could move on and build a relationship. But now he's probably dead and I'll have missed my chance."

"You don't know that for sure," Sal comments gently. "Don't give up hope just yet."

"I have hope," I reply. "But it's dwindling. You know how my life is. Things just never seem to work out in my favor. If not for you, I would be dead."

"Maybe that's the secret," he says suddenly.

I frown in confusion. "What do you mean?"

"You said you have bad luck. That your whole life is just bad luck. But maybe you need me to turn your luck around," he says, giving me a compassionate smile. I chuckle even as tears burn in my eyes.

"Maybe so," I agree. "But Sal, I'm so scared. I don't know where to go from here. What if my father is gone? What do we do? Blake is dead, but won't the police come sniffing around? And what about the mafia? How are you going to lay low? What if they find you?"

"Whoa, whoa. Those are questions for later on, Eva. Don't worry about that stuff right now. We have other things to worry about for the moment. Don't worry about me. I can handle myself, I promise. I've been in hotter situations than this before—I can work it out," he assures me. I'm not totally convinced, but at the moment, I have to trust him.

When we arrive at the hospital, the sun is just starting to peek over the horizon. The sky is gray and lilac, the air is cold and still. The snow has stopped falling and is now caked on the icy ground, making the world slippery. Sal and I are both pretty experienced with walking on ice, and still we have to move maddeningly slowly across the parking lot. It's infuriating, because I'm so impatient to just get into the hospital and go find my father.

Finally, we reach the entrance, and I take off down the hallway with Sal following close behind me. A nurse comes after us, shouting, "Stop! Where are you going? Security!"

Sal swivels around and gives her a venomous stare and she falls silent. We bolt for the elevator and take it up. I tap my foot impatiently the whole way up, and as soon as the doors part open I'm running again. I push past a nurse holding a stack of files and paperwork, causing her to lose her grip on the pile. Papers go flying everywhere and I wince, feeling terrible about it, but I can't stop moving now. I'm so close to my father's suite.

I look back over my shoulder and call out, "I'm so sorry!"

Sal is hot on my heels when I get to the hospital room door. It's locked.

"Sal, it's locked. It's locked. What do we do? I have to get in there!" I murmur frantically.

He looks around wildly, then makes a break for the nurses' station. He looks down at the young nurse at the desk and demands, "This young woman needs to see her father. He's gravely ill and we received word that he's in bad shape. Please let her in. Now"

The nurse looks taken aback by his request, frowning at him. "I'm afraid I don't know what you're talking about."

Sal's losing patience, I can tell. He points at me.

"This woman right here! Kirk Brighton is her father and he is in that hospital bed right now. Eva needs to see him before he... before he slips away. Do you understand?"

The nurse looks positively terrified of Sal, but she quickly hops up and grabs a set of keys from the desk, walking briskly over to the door where I'm waiting. My heart is racing and I can hardly breathe, terrified of what I might see when we get inside.

The nurse looks at me with utter confusion and says, "Your father is not dying, Miss. He's waking up." I blink a few times, not quite registering what she's said.

"He's... what?" Sal asks, stepping forward. The nurse takes a step back, clearly afraid of Sal. To be fair, he is pretty intimidating.

"Yes. Mr. Brighton stirred from his coma about

an hour ago. He's still not quite all there at the moment, but his vitals are good and he's been mumbling a name. 'Eva.' Still, you must be cautious and realistic in your expectations. Are you really his daughter?" she asks, biting her lip.

I nod. "Yes. I know I'm not his emergency contact, but I'm his daughter. I'm Eva."

She gives me a soft smile, tilting her head to one side slightly. "I can tell. You have his nose. I just never knew he even had a daughter."

"Nobody really does," I sigh. "Can I please go in and see him? I'll be gentle and patient, I swear. I just need to see him."

The nurse looks back and forth between Sal and me, sizing us up. Between my heartfelt plea and Sal's intimidating stare, she gives in. "Fine. But don't get him all riled up. He is definitely improving, but we don't want anything to knock him off-kilter."

"Got it," I say. "I promise."

"Okay," says the nurse. She unlocks the door and we burst inside. I walk up to my father's hospital cot, parting the curtain. At the sound of the curtains rustling, he finally opens his eyes. At first, he only squints at me in confusion.

"R-Rosemary?" he mumbles. My heart jolts at the sound of my mother's name.

I shake my head. "No, Dad. It's me, Eva. Your daughter."

His eyes go wide and a smile crosses his face. He

struggles to lift a hand, beckoning me to come closer and sit down next to him. I walk up and sit on the stool, taking his cold hand in mine. My father stares at me, his eyes charting my every feature as though he's trying to memorize my face.

"I can't believe you're really here," he mumbles in disbelief.

"Of course, I'm here," I tell him. "I had to see you."

"I hate that you have to see me this way," he says, a tear in his eye.

"It's not your fault. You're sick. It happens," I assure him.

"You are so kind," he says, staring at me. "I saw you in a dream, you know. While I was out. You were kind then, too."

"A dream?" I repeat.

"Yes. I dreamed that you came to see me. You told me that you wanted to forgive me," he adds. "A kindness I could never expect from you."

"That wasn't a dream," I tell him, my heart thumping. "I really did come to see you."

"How wonderful," he murmurs, smiling.

"Dad, a lot has happened while you were sleeping," I begin nervously. Sal steps forward from behind the curtain, and my father's eyes go wide. He looks between us, confused.

"Who is this young man?" he asks. I squeeze his hand reassuringly.

I brace myself, knowing that this next conversation is going to be a little rough. I have to tell him about Sal. And even worse, I have to tell him about Blake. But I just have to trust that my father can handle it. So I decide to just jump right in.

"I know this may not be the best time, but there's a lot I need to tell you."

The morning light that filters in through the church has never looked prettier. It lights up all the guests who sit in the pews, each one of them looking up at me and Eva at the altar.

I'm wearing a tuxedo that's blacker than black. There's a light touch of Italian cologne on me, my face is cleanly shaven, and I have a fresh haircut that made Eva's eyes light up as she watched my scruffy black hair fall away.

As for Eva, there's not an angel in heaven who could match up to her.

Her dress is whiter than the snow outside, hugging her form down to the hips and flaring out like an elegant swirl of clouds at her feet, and her hair hangs over one shoulder like a swirling golden gilding.

It's the same girl I saved what feels like a lifetime

ago, even though it's only been so little time. She's same girl who fell into my arms, the same girl who stood by me through more than I could have asked of anyone, much less someone with so much pain behind her. Her eyes have been watery since we saw each other on the aisle.

Her father walked by her side the whole way, healthy and beaming with joy at being allowed to have such an honor.

It's our wedding day, and I'm about to exchange vows with the most beautiful woman I've ever laid eyes on.

"Eva, my love," I say and the words are hardly out of my mouth before tears start running down her cheeks. "We met in one of the darkest times in my life and yours. I don't know what we did to deserve the chance to find each other. But when we did, Eva, we stepped out of darkness. And I never want to leave that light with you."

"Sal…" she starts, but she gets choked up before she can keep going. As she does, laughing at herself as she wipes a tear from her eye, I can't help but smile and feel my own eyes getting wetter.

There are sounds of sympathetic "Awws" from the audience of friends and family—mostly Eva's, but there are more than a few of my old friends watching us, and the room couldn't be fuller of warmth.

"Sal," she tries again, regaining her composure,

"before I met you, I didn't know what it meant to be vulnerable. You showed me how good that can be, both for me and for the people around me. I've grown because of you in ways I didn't know possible, and the walls I spent so much time building up are gone now. It feels better than I could have possibly dreamed. I love you, Salvatore, and I want to build something new with you for the rest of my life."

My heart is so swollen and overflowing at Eva's words that I can barely hear whatever it is the priest is saying. A tear rolls down my face, the first tear I can remember in a long, long time. In the background, I hear the words "You may now kiss the bride," and the words are hardly out of the priest's mouth before I seize Eva by the waist and pick her up.

Our lips press together with the applause of the audience, and I feel like fire is welling up in me. Her tears patter on my face as she holds my cheeks with her soft hands.

Soon after, we're rushing out the church to the cheers all around us, and down the steps of the church is the limousine, waiting and ready exactly as I arranged it.

Most of the people shouting good wishes and applauding for us are Eva's family, or rather, the family of her father.

As soon as I proposed to Eva, her father insisted

on the most lavish, beautiful wedding that Eva could have possibly wanted. And so, we found ourselves at a beautiful church in a "rustic" town upstate, on a day where fresh snow was covering the landscape in a blanket of beautiful, pristine white.

Kirk Brighton has a lot of making up to do for his daughter and everything she and her mother went through over their lives, but the wedding has been at least one solid step in the right direction.

Another step in the right direction is the protection his family's connections and power are able to give me to keep me hidden from the mafia. Those ties are long since cut, and while I'll still be watching my back for a long time for Eva's sake, the bulk of my worries are behind me. Fucking with Kirk Brighton's new son-in-law is a dangerous prospect, even for the mafia.

But from here on out, the honeymoon is on me, and I have a trip to Spain planned that Eva will never forget.

I help her into the limo, both of us grinning stupidly and piling in, waving to the crowds before the doors shut. With the partition to the driver's seat already closed, we're left in privacy at last, looking at each other with such passionate love that it makes me dizzy.

Alone together at last, just the way this all started.

"Did that just happen?" Eva asks, fluttering her eyes at me, and I can't help but laugh with her, taking her by the waist and bringing her in to pepper her face and her neck with kisses.

"Nobody ever remembers a thing about being up at the altar," I say. "That's what I hear, anyway. All I could focus on was you."

Her eyes get lidded, and she puts her arms around my shoulders, letting out a contented sigh. "This still doesn't feel real. All this is... it's more than a dream come true."

"Well, I have a few things that will make it feel more real, maybe," I say, cocking a smile.

She blushes, looking away for a moment and biting her lip before she says, "I think I do too, but you go first."

"When we were packing up your place," I say, thinking back to Eva's very modest living arrangements, "I noticed a few... things."

"Things?" she asks, cocking her head to the side.

"Mm, things that were missing."

She stares at me, trying to figure out what I mean.

"I've spoken with a few contacts of mine, and one of them has a sister who happens to be a cat breeder."

Eva's eyes start to get wider, her smile growing into a grin, but I hold her hands before she starts bouncing up and down excitedly.

"... and there *may* just be a litter of Ragdoll kittens

that's going to be born right around the time we get back from Spain."

"Ohmygodohmygodohmygod!" she gushes, kissing me excitedly all over, and I can't hold back my laughter for a few moments before I can get her to settle down.

"The second is something special," I say, and I reach into the compartment of the bar across from us in the limo. I take out a bottle of wine that looks jet-black, and the label is quite old. "I pulled a favor from an old friend of mine to get a bottle of wine straight from Sicily—one of the oldest vineyards in the country," I add with a smile. "Just for our wedding night."

She looks surprised, but there's something she isn't telling me on her lips—I know her well enough to be able to tell, easily. I furrow my eyebrows. "What's the matter?"

"I mean, it's fantastic!" she says nervously, "it's just that... we might want to save that for the anniversary."

I'm even more confused now. "Why?"

She holds back a smile. "I... won't be drinking alcohol for a little while."

I stare at her in complete confusion, but then it hits me, and it's my eyes' turn to widen. "Eva, do you mean...?"

"Sal, I'm pregnant," she says, her face positively glowing.

My heart races, and I feel as dizzy with happiness as I did the moment I picked her up at the altar a few moments ago. I seize her and kiss her deeply, then look her in the eye with a broad, sloppy grin on my face.

"Eva, this is wonderful!" I say, "We're going to be parents!" This kind of joy isn't like me, but seeing my wife there—*my wife!*—and knowing that we're going to bring a new life into the world fills me with something new and beautiful.

And the very next moment, I press Eva back against the seat with a deep, long kiss, letting my tongue delve into her as I grope her breast through her unbelievably expensive wedding dress.

She gasps at first, then moans into the kiss, putting her hand over mine and sighing in delight at the feeling.

I pull her on top of me and pull her in close. The limo is large and spacious, and she has plenty of room to get positioned the way she wants. She starts pushing her hips into me, a soft moan with each little thrust as we kiss each other sloppily.

My hands touch every part of her they can get their hands on. They squeeze her ass, run up and down the bare back exposed by her dress, grip her hair and tilt her head back just enough to ravage her neck with kisses.

I press my lips to the nape of her neck and just

hold them there for a few long, beautiful moments as I hug her to me.

The next moment, I pull her shoes off and hitch her dress up. She gasps and looks down at me in alarm. "Right here? Are you sure?"

"When am I not?" I growl, and with one hand I pull her neck down to me so I can silence her lips with a kiss. The other hand works up her legs to her underwear. I tug at it at first, but I soon lose patience.

"After everything you've been through," I say in a low, husky tone, "you deserve nothing but the best, Eva. And for the rest of your life, I'm going to make that happen."

I unbutton my pants, and I let my cock spring forth from my tuxedo, feeling it touch the warmth of Eva's pussy. I grind her against me slowly at first. She's wet, but I want her wetter. It takes almost no time at all for me to start feeling her slickness on my cock.

"We're going to ruin our clothes," she says with a laugh as I keep going, able to hold her up easily with arms like tree trunks.

"Nobody has to know," I say with a dark chuckle. "I won't tell if you don't." I lean in and whisper into her ear, "But I can't promise I'll be gentle."

Her whole body shivers, and when I feel her wet enough for me, I slide her onto my cock, right there in the limo.

I hold my bride in both hands and thrust up into her in a steady rhythm, but both of us are almost delirious with pounding hearts and racing blood.

Eva grips the seat behind me for support as I use her, feeling her tight, smooth pussy, groaning as my whole body comes alive at that life-giving touch.

I've loved Eva for longer than I've admitted to myself, but being in touch with her in the most literal way brings me into a state that's unlike any other. Suits and formal outfits always feel tight and uncomfortable on me, but with Eva wrapped around my cock, I feel truly free.

She presses her lips into me as I fuck her, feeling her warmth running down my cock and wetting my balls while each hard pounding up into her makes them touch her lower lips.

The thought that I got her pregnant makes me solid as a rock, and the emotions coursing through both of us make it all the sweeter when I start to feel my bride tighten and get closer and closer to the edge.

She starts to cry out when her orgasm hits, but I grab her and silence her with a kiss, feeling her beautiful moan in my chest while I let myself spill over into orgasm.

My cock throbs as I shoot hot seed into her, the first time as husband and wife, barely a few minutes after being declared official.

My cock is still unloading into her wet, needy

pussy when I bring her close and whisper into her ear, "How does it feel, Mrs. Angelo?"

She gasps as a sudden shiver of delight runs up her back at the sound of the name, and she collapses onto me while our orgasms subside together.

After blissful moments of stillness together with nothing but our breathing and heartbeats to listen to, she pushes herself up on my shoulders and looks at me with those eyes I feel blessed to be able to look into forever, and those soft lips smile.

"It feels like forever."

Rock Hard Bodyguard

Abducted

Vegas Boss

I Hired A Hitman

Killing For Her

The Assassin's Heart

Romance:

Falling for her Boss (Novella)

Most Wanted: Lilly (Novella)

Bound as the World Burns (SFF)

Erotic Thriller:

THE DANGEROUS MEN SERIES:

The Narrow Path

Strayed from the Path

Path to Ruin

ABOUT THE AUTHOR

 Alexis Abbott is a Wall Street Journal & USA Today bestselling author who writes about bad boys protecting their girls! Pick up her books today if you can't resist a bad boy who is a good man, and find yourself transported with super steamy sex, gritty suspense, and lots of romance.

She lives in beautiful St. John's, NL, Canada with her amazing husband.